The Philadelphia Inquirer

A Christmas Quartet

Four modern tales
of the holiday

By Chris Satullo

Illustrations by Tony Auth

Books by The Philadelphia Inquirer

Lost at Sea:
The Atlantic Claims 10 Men
By Douglas A. Campbell

Crisis on the Coast:
The Risky Development of America's Shore
By Gilbert M. Gaul and Anthony R. Wood

Beyond the Flames:
One toxic dump, two decades of sorrow
By Susan Q. Stranahan and Larry King

Philly's Final Four
UConn Rocks the Cradle of Women's Basketball
By the staff of The Inquirer

FAQs:
Sounds answers to real computing questions
By John J. Fried

ISBN 1-58822-004-4

© Copyright 2000 by The Philadelphia Inquirer. All rights reserved. No part of this book may be reproduced by any electronic or mechanical means including information and retreival systems without permission in writing from The Philadelphia Inquirer except by a reviewer who may quote brief passages in a review.

Table of Contents

Introduction 5

The Innkeeper's Tale 9

Josh Sees the Light 41

The Nick of Time 57

A Christmas Carol@mega-ware.com 81

To Eileen, Sara and Matt
— *C.S.*

To Katie and Emily
— *T.A.*

Introduction

It was Tony Auth's fault.

As is our habit, we were sitting around one morning in his office (much nicer than mine; how'd that happen?) discussing the state of the universe and what The Inquirer ought to say about it in its next issue.

And Tony, whose skill as a cartoonist is exceeded only by his worth as a friend, said, "You know, we ought to do something together. You write a story and I'll illustrate it."

It was November. The Salvation Army Santas were already tolling their bells outside the mall entrance, waiting to hear something rattle in the kettle. Kids had already been driven into a frenzy of greedy anticipation by the commercials jammed inside Power Rangers episodes.

So a Christmas story it had to be. Something modern, with some fun to it, but also with a message — spiritual but not overtly religious, suitable for framing inside a mass-market daily newspaper.

As is my habit, so exasperating to those around me, my creative efforts began with a pun. Shepard – my protagonist's name would be a weak wordplay on those bit players in the Christmas story. Who might be the modern equivalent of those ancient, minimum-wage, night-shift workers? Hmmm. Of course! A gas station-minimart clerk, tending over his flock of TastyKakes. Which gas station? Why not the one by the Blue Route that I cut through each night on the way home from work to avoid that darn endless red light?

From there, it was just a few short, silly, enjoyable hops to "Josh Sees the Light," which first saw the light of day on Christmas Eve 1996. Enough people liked it that Tony and I agreed to try another tale.

In 1997, seeing that a retelling of the indispensable Dickens was inevitable, we decided to get it over with. Any fool with Microsoft Word loaded onto his PC would have had the sense to update Scrooge as a gazillionaire software mogul. "A Christmas Carol@mega-ware.com" had folks telling us they loved seeing the serial yarn revived in the daily paper. And Tony and I were hooked on the pleasures of producing them.

By Christmastime 1998, the dispiriting Clinton scandals had us all yearning for a release into fantasy. The ultimate Yuletide fantasy hero, Santa Claus, beckoned. But, in line with the glum times, he turned out to be a burned-out

St. Nick in need of salvation himself. Readers seemed to relish "The Nick of Time" as a redemptive break from the news of impeachment.

By 1999, even someone as dim as I had figured out that each one of these tales hinged on a similar theme: How can you balance the demands of modern, consumerist life with the spiritual yearning for redemption embodied by the Christmas story? And what character in the Christmas narrative better exemplifies that tension than the stressed-out innkeeper who manages to do the right thing? Presto, out came "The Innkeeper's Tale," set in a region where I long lived and where a piece of my heart still resides, the Lehigh Valley.

The response of readers to these little tales has been gratifying. Equally so has been the experience of collaborating with a prince of the realm like Tony Auth. I am also indebted to John Timpane, a shining North Star of an editor if ever there was one. Thanks also to colleagues Kevin Ferris and Cindy Henry, who copy-edited these tales and displayed them on the page with consummate professionalism, and to Jane R. Eisner, who as editor of the Editorial Board in 1996, supported our little experiment, and to Dick Cooper, who agreed to put these words inside a cover, if only to shut me up.

Thanks above all to my wife of 21 long-suffering years, Eileen, and our children, Sara and Matt. The three of them tolerate in good humor the long hours and crazed demeanor of an author in the heat of composition, however minor and silly the words that result. And that, my friends, is love you can't buy.

—*Chris Satullo*

The Innkeeper's Tale

Carol 1: O Little Town of Bethlehem

Tshaka Steward strolled across the fragrant, dowdy lobby of Excelsior's Inn at Bethlehem, past a row of evergreens swathed in serene loops of white light.

From a balcony above the front doors, the Virgin Mary, Joseph and the Magi gazed down at him — along with the other sturdy wooden figures of the inn's manger scene.

Hand-carved, 80 years old, a Bethlehem tradition — Tshaka could quote by heart from the brochure the hotel sent out, trying to lure for a night's stay some of the tourists drawn to Pennsylvania's Christmas City by its gorgeous lights, holiday market and live Christmas pageant.

At the door, Tshaka eased aside to let pass two men wearing shepherd's garb nearly identical to that of one figure in the creche above. They were actors from the pageant, whose final performance had concluded minutes before. Cast members were straggling in clumps up the hill from the arts pavilion, drawn to the mellow warmth and strong spirits waiting in the hotel's lobby bar.

Tshaka stepped outside to check the weather, while wrestling with the lust for nicotine. Since he'd gotten the manager's job at the inn, he'd become, to his disgust, a pack-a-day man. The habit had cranked into overdrive after Jacqui had phoned him to say that she and the kids wouldn't be accompanying him on the transfer from Philadelphia, that he'd best get himself a place in the Lehigh Valley. "No need to drive all the way to Germantown after one of your 12-hour days just to turn around and drive back for another one," she'd said in a voice like an icestorm.

"God rest ye merry, gentlemen . . ." Across Main Street, a group of carolers stood, bundled and rosy-cheeked, by the Moravian Bookstore, their melody surging and fading with the wind.

Tshaka glanced skyward, past the cupola of Central Moravian Church. The forecast — *Condition WHITE! Heavy snow with drifts* — looked accurate. The skies, knotted and leaden, seemed to slump low enough to touch. Tshaka tried, then dropped his arm. He shuddered. The

dream had come again last night, spawning the funk that had dogged him through this long, bad day:

He was lying on his back, looking at a night sky bristling with stars. Rapt, he reached up to them, but his hand slammed into an invisible barrier, bending backward at the wrist. Panic rising, he felt around himself. Glass above, beside, below, behind him. A coffin of glass. He could see his breath. It was frosting over the glass, blotting out the stars. He tried not to breathe but instead panted faster. Intricate latticeworks of ice formed on the glass. He was on his back, panting, in a dark world of ice.

"Above thy deep and dreamless sleep, the silent sta-a-a-rs go by . . ." The carolers' tune yanked him from his reverie. Snowflakes had begun to fall. Tshaka Steward shivered, swore off a smoke, and returned to the warm, burbling lobby of his hotel.

His hotel. It was a lovable ol' gal, trim and proud. Her elegance had faded since the days when the blast furnaces on the far bank of the Lehigh River had roared all day and night, the days when Bethlehem Steel had ruled the valley, luring a stream of pin-striped suits to the inn's chandeliered conference rooms and its smoky bar to make deals.

Now, the Inn at Bethlehem was but a minor bauble in the Excelsior chain's trove of assets. Still, Tshaka was glad enough to have it vouchsafed to him. Oh, they'd made a fuss of what they'd done, the sleek vice presidents in their tasseled loafers, when they'd given him the reins in Bethlehem. First African American to run an Excelsior! Up from entry-level clerk in just 12 years! What a tribute to our wisdom! What a credit to his . . . well, never mind. The sleek men knew enough to stop short of gross cliche.

Did they also, Tshaka thought ruefully, know how to

make a glass ceiling look like an open door? Was this job, at a troubled property in a scuffling town, a rung on the ladder — or a trapdoor?

Inside, Tshaka looked over to the bar, trying to draw cheer from its comical bustle. Shepherds, wise men, angels, the whole motley crew of Nativity myth milled about the high stools and overstuffed chairs, clapping backs, raising toasts and noisily saluting another smashing

Bethlehem Live Christmas Pageant. More real animals in the cast and more out-of-towners in the audience than ever, that morning's Express-Times had announced.

The scene lifted Tshaka for a millisecond, before a sour thought: "I hope we don't 86 on the Chivas Regal, too." That had been the middle of his bad day, when a tour bus had unexpectedly descended upon the hotel restaurant at lunch, causing it to run out — "to 86" in hotelier's parlance — of shrimp, prime rib and arugula.

What else had gone awry on this second-to-last shopping day before Christmas?

The flu bug had buzzed through his staff, leaving the 160-room inn shorthanded. He'd been forced to put Jen, a trainee, at the front desk for much of the afternoon, with dire results. Jen just couldn't get it through her head to hit the "refresh" icon on her computer screen periodically to make sure the room inventory shown there was updated with other clerks' entries.

The upshot? Twice she'd blithely sent guests off with encoded electronic keys to rooms already occupied. The first time was a minor glitch. The second was cataclysmic, since the original guests had been, as the duplicate guest delicately put it, "amorously engaged" when he clumped into the room, suitcase in tow.

To calm the fiasco, Tshaka had to comp both parties their rooms for the night.

"Just what my Rev-PAR needs," Tshaka sighed, swinging behind the registration desk to head for his tiny office. Revenue per available room — in spare moments this day, Tshaka had been trying to calculate how that key measure of hotel performance was running in the final quarter, in preparation for what he was sure was an impending visit from Giles Stone, his regional vice president.

Stone never announced his "drive-by shootings," as the gallows wit of the chain's junior managers labeled them. He was notorious for showing up before holidays, in the middle of tourist crushes, or smack on the weekend when the manager's in-laws had flown in from Omaha.

Tshaka, just six months on the job at a problematic property, knew he had to be in Stone's holiday sights. He settled behind his cluttered desk to fiddle with a spreadsheet.

Minutes later, Jen's flushed face poked into his office: "Mr. Steward, I have a kind of a situation out here. Maybe you could come out?"

Yep, Tshaka thought, he'd have to help work the desk all night. No getting out of here before 11 tonight. Might just have to spend another night in one of the guest rooms, rather than fighting through that snow to his little place in Catasauqua.

Tshaka glided out to the desk, all crisp competence.

On the other side of the desk stood two young people, grim, wet, bedraggled. The young man was slim, handsome, with a coal-black mustache and goatee, to which clung the sparkling remains of a dozen snowflakes. On his head he wore a red do-rag, in his right ear a gold earring, and on his back a thin, satin warm-up jacket. The young woman had brown eyes that, even rimmed in weariness as they were, sent an arrow of adrenaline through Tshaka's gut.

She was pregnant, very pregnant, standing splay-footed as she rubbed her enormous belly through her Eagles sweatshirt and looked beseechingly at the handsome man in the blue blazer who'd just come out to decide her fate.

"This is Jose Carpintero and Maria Encarnacion," Jen said precisely, as though hosting a cocktail party.

"Ms. Encarnacion has just come from St. Luke's Hospital, where they were sent away. They would like a room for the night."

Tshaka leaned close to Jen and whispered, "Well, then, why don't we give them a room?"

"They have no credit card," Jen blurted. "And nowhere near enough cash."

Tshaka glanced at the couple. Behind their heads, the figures in the lobby creche gazed down at him. Jose. Maria. Pregnant. Christmas. The Inn.

"Good Lord," Tshaka sighed.

Carol 2: Let Every Heart Prepare Him Room

Tshaka Steward gazed at the wet and anxious couple on the other side of the front desk.

On this, already the worst day of Tshaka's six months of running the place, Jose Carpintero and Maria Encarnacion wanted a room at the inn. Though the inn's lobby bustled with holiday clatter, rooms were available. That wasn't the problem. The young people were.

They had no credit card, and nowhere near enough cash for the double-the-rate deposit that Excelsior hotel chain policy demanded for those foolish enough to leave home without it. Besides, they looked more like they'd run to the Wawa for an Icee than to a three-star hotel for a stay — he in his do-rag, earring and warm-up jacket, she in her Eagles sweatshirt and leggings. The tale of woe they offered had the distinct scent of a con.

But young Maria truly was pregnant, no mistaking that. She looked weary, scared and achingly beautiful as she slumped into a wing chair in the lobby, rubbing her belly.

Compassion and common sense began a rousing tug of war, using Tshaka's stomach as the rope.

Leading the cheers for compassion in Tshaka's mind was old Pastor Isaac Roush, lion of Grace Deliverance Church back in Philly, who surely knew how to bring the news:

"Ahhh, yes, I'd love to be there, brothers and sisters, the day when you make your alibis to Jee-sus. 'But, Lord, how were we supposed to know that was You pushing that grocery cart, reeking of 20-20? How were we supposed to know You were that skinny boy down on the corner, waiting for someone decent to take him under his wing, before the drug gang did?' And the Loooord will say, 'Did you expect I'd send a telegram to tell you the hour I was coming? Did you expect me to announce it on KYW?' The Lord will shake his head in wonder: 'Did you expect me to send you an eeee-mail? Didn't I give you the Good Book so you'd know to look for me in the low place as well as the high? Didn't I warn you, brothers and sisters, that you wouldn't know the hour or the place? Didn't I?'"

But common sense had its own gospel, preached sternly in Tshaka's mind by one Giles Stone, regional vice president of the chain, who might, in fact, show up in the flesh at any moment: "Our product is our reputation. Never cheat the product, never risk the reputation."

"Mr. Carpintero," Tshaka began, "please review your situation again for me."

"I came up from Philly today, you know, Kensington?"

"I'm Germantown, myself."

"No way! Really? Well, then you know what a crazy road that 309 is. I got this old Chevy and those tires, sheesh ... Way it's snowing out there, I could fishtail right into a semi. I can't risk that. I can't risk our baby. Can't you help us?"

Pay for a cab, common sense counseled. Send them to

the Motel 6 on Route 22. Just get their scruffy faces out of your lobby.

"I'm up here for a job interview," Jose went on, campaigning. "My man at the unemployment sent me up. I've got a trade, you know, printing. Had a good job but somebody bought the company and, POW, laid off! Maria came, see, 'cause she grew up in Bethlehem, and she was excited to see the lights again."

A job interview? In those clothes? Actually, Tshaka didn't doubt it. Dealing in entry-level service jobs as he did, he'd interviewed dozens of sincere people, many of whom turned out to be solid workers, who hadn't had a clue how to present themselves in the working world.

"So after I talked to the man at the plant, we drove around a bit looking at the lights, then Maria" — Jose glanced at her with tenderness — "started having pains,

you know? I saw a hospital sign so we went up the hill over there." He gestured vaguely.

"St. Luke's," Tshaka offered.

"Yeah, that's it. So they hooked Maria up with these wires, but then they said it was a false alarm, Brassy Licks, or somethin'."

"Braxton-Hicks," Tshaka corrected. He'd been the male star of two Lamaze classes, totally into the lingo of cleansing breaths and dilation. Sweet recollection sluiced across his mind: Roderick and Lauryn as pink-mouthed, brown-skinned newborns. Eight and 5, they were now. A knot of pain shoved aside the sweetness. He toted up the days since he'd seen them, since Jacqui had declared the separation. God, would he even see them at Christmas?

"Yeah, yeah, Braxton-Hicks, so they sent us home. But I got a feeling those docs are wrong. I got a feeling this maybe is her time. I'm scared to drive her over that mountain in this blizzard. You understand, right? You can help us, right?"

"Well, it would be highly irregular. . ." the words, tasting like tin in Tshaka's throat, petered out.

"Please, bro. When I saw you come out, I told myself, 'With this guy, we got a chance.' Thought you might keep it real, not just act like The Man, you know."

There it was: the old, sharp-edged card, right on the table. Which side you on, homeboy?

Tshaka looked up at the figures in the manger scene in the balcony above the entrance. He looked at Maria, whose head leaned back, eyes closed, as she exhaled slowly. Her eyes opened and looked at him, brown and round.

Common sense tumbled into the pit, a loser.

"OK," Tshaka said, reaching for his own wallet. "MasterCard it is. We'll take an impression here to cover your charges, then show you to the room. Jen, let's give these good people Room 313."

Wide-eyed, Jen ran the key card through the encoder. Tshaka made it to the wing chair in time to steady one of Maria's arms as Jose lifted her gently to her feet.

"Jerry!" The wizened bellhop had been humping suitcases through this lobby since God was a pup. "Jerry, please take these folks up to 313. No baggage. Once they're settled, please pick up a full set of toiletries from the hotel store and deliver it to the room. Charge it to my account."

"Yes, sir!" Jerry neatly herded the two toward the elevator.

Tshaka trudged to his office. Hope the auditors don't question this one. His phone signaled a message waiting. The recorded voice was gruff, familiar:

"Steward, Giles Stone here. I'm on my way to your

property, but it's slow going because no one in this damn state knows how to drive in snow. Should be there about 6. Have the monthly reports ready."

Tshaka punched "star-D" to delete the message. If only life had the same feature ...

His face slid into his splayed hands.

"Good Lord," he said.

Carol 3: Let Nothing Ye Dismay

The printer in Tshaka Steward's office whirred and clicked, spitting out the rows of figures and charts that the young hotel manager was rushing to pull together to appease Stone, due to arrive at any moment.

Tshaka strolled into the lobby, where a festive mood to match the inn's elaborate decorations was growing. The bank Christmas party was gobbling hors d'oeuvres in the Zinzendorf Room. Cast members from the City of Bethlehem's Live Christmas Pageant, still attired as shepherds, Wise Men and whatnot, were wassailing and caroling lustily in the lobby bar.

A red-cheeked guest clomped up to the front desk, shaking snow off a wide-brimmed hat. "It's coming down like the Dickens out there," he said.

The young couple he'd just put up in Room 313 might have been right, Tshaka thought: It probably would have been foolhardy to drive a pregnant woman back to Philadelphia in this storm.

Tshaka, trim in his blue Excelsior chain blazer, closed his eyes and inhaled deeply, hoping the scent of evergreen and the sounds of merriment would wash away his inner funk. What a day, full of stress: the flu bug that decimated his staff, the resulting room-service and room-assignment screwups, the impending arrival of the flinty Stone, the dicey decision to let that couple with no credit card or money camp in 313.

Underlying it all was the drumbeat of despair in his heart over Jacqui and the kids. Would she relent and let them spend Christmas together, or was this "separation" a euphemism for something more dire?

Suddenly, his ears detected something new in the noise from the bar, a different timbre, one of anger. He opened his eyes just in time to see one Wise Man shove another into the back of a wing chair. The second of the soused Magi gathered himself, then lunged at the other with a wild swing, yelling, "You stole that commission from me, you $#&*@*!"

In the seconds that it took Tshaka to stride across the lobby, a shepherd and an angel had managed to separate the combatants. Tshaka recognized one as John Hennessey, a real estate agent he'd met at a Chamber breakfast. He didn't plan to waste time finding out who the other guy was.

"John," Tshaka said soothingly, palms up, looking into Hennessey's flushed visage. "Let's chill, OK, friend? Let's not spoil the holiday mood. I'll call you a cab, OK?"

He looked at the robed revelers holding each drunken pugilist by the arms.

"I'll get two cabs. Can one of you go with John and someone with this other gentleman?"

"Sure, Tshaka, no problem," said an angel whom he suddenly recognized as the manager of the bookstore across the street.

"Good. I'll make the calls," Tshaka said, turning to go, then felt his heart nose-dive to his loafers.

Giles Stone stood just inside the front door, brushing snow off his camel coat and taking in the tableau with wry menace.

Tshaka hustled over.

"Mr. Stone, glad you made it through the storm!"

"What are you running here, Steward, a biker bar?" Stone asked through an icy smile.

Tshaka clutched Stone's elbow.

"Let me take you back to the office," he said.

Before they could take a step, John the doorman peeked his head in the door: "Mr. Steward, sir, you've got to come see this!"

Excusing himself, Tshaka stepped outside, where a curtain of fat, moist snowflakes was beginning to drape a white mantle across Main Street's signature lampposts.

"Look! Down there!" the doorman said, pointing toward the Hill-to-Hill Bridge.

A clump of snowballs with legs was moving up the sidewalk toward the hotel, a high-pitched bark emerging from somewhere behind the pack.

What the ?!!

It took a second for Tshaka's brain to sort out the incongruous scene. Those were sheep, a half-dozen or so, and that was Hardy, Miss Minerva Watson's Shetland sheepdog, his leash trailing in the snow, herding them frantically up Main Street. In the distance, Tshaka could see Miss Watson, slipping and waving her arms as she struggled up the wet sidewalk, far behind Hardy.

As the Express-Times would report the next day, Miss Watson had been giving Hardy his usual walk through the historic industrial quarter down the hill from the hotel, where Tshaka had often exchanged hellos with her while taking a cigarette break. The sheep, the hooved stars of the Live Christmas Pageant's manger scene, had just been herded into a truck for transport back to a farm near Bath when the truck skidded and slammed into a tree.

That stunned the driver and knocked down the truck's back gate. The sheep, finding themselves on the ground, huddled there until Hardy caught sight of them. His genes on fire, Hardy pulled free of old Miss Watson's grasp and began doing what Shelties do, herding the flock up the hill and up Main Street.

They were about even with the hotel awning now.

Behind him, Tshaka heard Stone's voice: "Steward, what is . . . ?"

When Stone opened that door, a light clicked on in the sheep's dim brains: *Warm! Pen! Must go!* With Hardy

nipping at its rear, the woolly phalanx made a sudden left toward the open door as Tshaka cried out, "Mr. Stone, no!"

Stone's face morphed in a millisecond from indignation to terror as the woolly clump surged by, knocking him back into the lobby and into a prickly evergreen. Appalled, Tshaka had the presence of mind to lunge and grab Hardy's leash before the dog could follow the flock through the door. He handed Hardy over to the doorman and raced inside.

Over at the lobby bar, laughter pealed, fingers pointed. Tshaka caught a glimpse of Jen, the young desk clerk, looking stricken, then followed her eyes to the spot near the grand staircase where the sheep's momentum had run out. They huddled together there, looking sublimely stupid.

"Steward! Steward, you moron!" Giles Stone's voice sliced through the laughter. "Help me up!"

Stone slumped awkwardly against a Christmas tree that had itself teetered back against a wall. He fumbled to get his right arm untangled from a string of white lights. A welt on his left cheek testified to a close encounter with a tree branch.

Pine needles showed on the shoulder of his camel coat and blind fury on his face.

"Good Lord," Tshaka murmured.

Carol 4: We Three Kings of Orient Are

It was a multiple-choice test you'd never see in hotel-management school. But Tshaka Steward, surveying the chaos in the lobby of his Inn at Bethlehem, had to get it right in the next five seconds.

The quiz: Six sheep are huddled moronically in the lobby of your hotel, by the grand staircase. Your boss, meanwhile, having just been knocked down by said sheep, is doing an angry tango with a Christmas tree. Which do you tend to first — A) the sheep or B) the boss?

Correct answer: B. Tshaka, who hadn't become the first African American to run an Excelsior hotel by being dim, got it right. He lifted Giles Stone up, brushed needles off his camel coat and murmured reassuringly, like a mom coaxing a toddler into a snowsuit.

"Steward!!!!" In his rage, those were the only syllables Stone could muster.

Over at the lobby bar, revelers clad as Wise Men and shepherds — cast members from the just-concluded Live Christmas Pageant, which had starred the now lobby-bound sheep — doubled over in laughter at Stone and the sheep. "You're shepherds. Do something," Tshaka thought, illogically.

"Take me to your office," Stone hissed.

Tshaka turned that grim task over to Jen, the young clerk, then punched a number into the phone at the front desk.

"Engineering. Lou," came a prompt reply.

"Lou, Tshaka. We got a problem you wouldn't believe in the lobby."

"Really? I was just going to call you about the problem we got by the loading dock. You won't believe this, either."

"What is it, Lou?"

"Don't know how to tell you this, boss, but we got a camel down by the Dumpster. He ain't happy, and he ain't moving. Spat at Herman when he tried to come close."

Tshaka laughed. He couldn't help it. "I'll see your camel and raise you six sheep."

"Huh?"

"There's six sheep standing in the lobby. They just knocked Giles Stone over."

"Stone's here? Well, Lord bless me and keep me. What

we got going on here, boss, that Robin Williams flick *Jujube*, or what?"

"*Jumanji*," Tshaka sighed. One of Lauryn's favorites, he'd given it to the kids two Christmases ago. This Christmas, for a family on the road to breakup, wouldn't be so sweet. "Lou, I think the Live Pageant must have had a jailbreak. Let's do this: Have Herman stand sentry on Joe Camel. You get up here pronto. Bring a broom or something to use as a shepherd's staff, and we'll herd them onto the freight elevator and down to the dock. Gather our livestock in one place, you know? Then I'll call the pageant director, the county extension service, whoever I can get to help.

"And, Lou, bring some air freshener. I never knew sheep stank like this."

Unlike most things on this, the worst day of Tshaka's hotel career, his plan worked smoothly. Lou showed an unsuspected knack for animal wrangling, getting the sheep clear of the lobby before any of them left unseemly deposits on the rug. The police, having responded to the truck accident down the hill that had let the animals loose, tracked the beasts to the hotel and restored them to their owners.

A half-hour later, Tshaka was back in the lobby, relieved. Then it hit him: Giles Stone! He'd left his boss bruised and stewing in the office, no doubt poring over the inn's fiscal reports, which Tshaka ardently wished had been a little rosier.

"Mr. Steward?" Jen hailed him, her voice edged in panic. "I'm so, so sorry, sir, but I have another . . . situation?"

"What now, Jen?"

She gestured at three young men at the front desk, all with ball caps on backward and pants so baggy that Berber tribesmen could make a tent out of the material.

"They want to see the folks in 313" — young Jose and his pregnant girlfriend, Maria, whom Tshaka had given a room even though they had no credit.

"Yo! What up?" said the middle one of the three, a redhead. "Can we see Maria and Jose, or what?"

"And you are . . . ?"

"We're friends of Maria from her old neighborhood. I'm Mel, he [black hair] is Gaspar, and that [blonde hair falling to the waist] is Baldy."

"What's in the bags?"

"Jose called and asked us to bring some stuff. Maria needs baby oil, he says, for massage. We brought some smokes for Jose and . . . " — Mel pulled out a wad of bills — "some dead presidents. Jose said you were a nice guy. He didn't want to jam you up, so he asked us to bring some dough to pay for the room. I got 80 bucks. That do it?"

30   THE PHILADELPHIA INQUIRER

Tshaka had to smile. What the heck, in for a dime . . . "Rooms are $150 a night," he said. "But don't worry about it; this one's on me.

"And, Mel, I can understand why Jose needs a drag, believe me, but the room's no smoking. So, only outside. Understand?"

Mel grinned, hands spread in a "Who, me?" gesture. "Hey, bro," he said, "never around a baby."

"Well, there's no baby yet," Tshaka said. "You can take that elevator over there."

As Mel, Gaspar and Baldy waited for the elevator, Tshaka idly noted the backs of their caps. The team logos: the Kansas City Royals, the L.A. Kings, the Orlando Magic.

Tshaka went to his office. Stone was busily marking up printouts. "Sit, Steward," he said, not looking up. "I have questions."

Jen, voice trembling, poked her head in.

"Mr. Steward, it's Jose in 313! He said the baby's coming! Maria's water broke! Bring towels, he said, lots of tow-

els!"
   Stone looked up, eyebrows arched.
   "Good Lord," Tshaka whispered.

Carol 5: What Child Is This?

"You did WHAT?" Giles Stone's face was so red that the welt put there an hour before by an errant Christmas tree branch hardly stood out.

Tshaka Steward's lifelong habit of honesty had often proved troublesome policy. This time, he thought ruefully, he'd gone beyond candor to folly.

His only excuse was that it had been quite an unsettling hour on the job as manager of the Inn at Bethlehem. He'd broken up a scuffle between two drunken "wise men," survived a visitation of his lobby by a flock of sheep, and now was trying to help a scared 19-year-old with heart-stopping eyes who'd begun labor in room 313.

It was on this last point — the bedraggled, broke couple from Philadelphia in 313 — that Tshaka had just given his agitated regional boss, Giles Stone, way more information than he should have. Why had he told Stone that, as an act of mercy, he'd let two young people with no credit card get a room — in violation of Excelsior chain policy?

He'd had to explain why he needed to attend immediately to the crisis in 313 that Jen, the young front-desk clerk, had just announced. Somehow, the whole story of his attack of compassion tumbled out.

"It's not bad enough, Steward, that in my first five minutes here I witness a drunken brawl and get caught in a stampede of barnyard animals. Now, I find out you've turned an Excelsior hotel into a homeless shelter. Reputation is all, Steward, and by letting in these type of people, you damage the Excelsior name."

"What kind of people is that, exactly, sir?"

"Oh, don't get politically correct with me, mister. You're in enough trouble as it is."

Tshaka looked into his boss' wrathful eyes. He felt a door slide open inside his soul, felt himself march through it.

"I'm going to check on this poor woman," he said evenly, "then get her a ride to a hospital. *These people* will be out of the hotel shortly."

It wasn't to be. Tshaka hustled up to 313. Maria lay propped up on the bed, panic in her eyes, as Jose stroked her cheek. Their friend Mel was busily rinsing and hanging towels in the bathroom; his friends, Gaspar and Baldy, were flipping through channels on the TV, with the sound off.

"I'll get my car to take you to St. Luke's," he called out.

"Hurry," Maria murmured.

The swirling snow stung Tshaka's face as he brushed off his Accord's windshield. The parking lot was down an incline from Main Street. Rushing, Tshaka tried to gun it up the hill. The car shimmied, then skidded, careening into a large drift. The wheels spun fecklessly. No traction. He

was stuck.

Furious at himself, he raced back to 313. Maria was moaning, while Jose chattered, "WhatshouIdowhatshouldIdo?" Gaspar and Baldy turned from "Wheel of Fortune" to stare at Maria as she screamed, "I hate this pain!" Mel came out of the bathroom with a wet wash rag and dabbed her face.

Tshaka sized up the situation. "Jose, Maria, did you have childbirth classes?"

"No, Maria just wanted to have the drugs. She hates pain."

"Understood," Tshaka exhaled sharply. "Gaspar, Baldy — go down to the bar and have a drink. On me. Mel, you stay. Got a watch? Good. I want you to time the period between the end of this contraction and the next, OK? Jose, just hold her hand."

Tshaka dialed 911, explained the situation, asked for an ambulance. The dispatcher replied there'd just been a six-car wreck on Route 22 — a bad one, injuries, Jaws of Life. It might be a while before a crew got clear. "How long between contractions?" the dispatcher asked. Tshaka signaled Mel, who held up three fingers.

"Three minutes? Yikes!" dispatcher said. "Know how to deliver a baby, sir?"

"Watched my two get born, Lamaze," Tshaka said.

"That may have to do. I'll try to hustle some paramedics over there."

The techniques and lingo Tshaka had crammed into his brain proudly during childbirth training wormed their way up from memory.

Putting his face inches from Maria's, he said, "OK, Maria, dear, I'm going to teach you some tricks I know to help with the pain. I just need you to listen and concentrate; I know it's hard, but try."

As quickly, gently, simply as he could, Tshaka explained Lamaze breathing. Maria just stared up at him, pleadingly. He had an idea: "Maria, you love the Christmas lights here, right?" She nodded. Without taking his eyes off hers, he called out, "Mel, in the hallway, there's a photo of a Moravian star. Go get it."

When Mel returned, Tshaka told him to hold the framed image in Maria's line of sight. "Now, Maria, when the pain starts to come, I want you to look at nothing but the star, think of nothing but the star, put your mind inside the star. The pain will be somewhere else, but you'll be safe inside the star. OK?"

So it went for two hours, as the contractions swept over Maria in waves, Jose stroking her face, Mel holding the photo of the star, Tshaka coaching, coaxing, soothing. Between contractions, he called 911 over and over, until the dispatcher said, "Tshaka, hang on. I've got one on the way."

Minutes passed. Maria shouted at Jose, "Get your hands off me!" Jose reared back, wounded. Maria yelled, "Ohgodohgodohgod, it hurts so bad!" There was scant

interval between waves of pain now. *In transition*, Tshaka thought grimly.

Puffing his cheeks comically, Tshaka tried to show Maria how to "he-blow," the staccato exhales that ease the urge to push.

Suddenly, Maria howled. "It's COMING! Get it out of MEEE! I need to PUSH!!!!!!!!"

Jose's face wheeled to Tshaka. It was streaked with tears. "Mr. Steward?" he implored.

"Mel, get me some hot water and more towels," Tshaka said evenly. He didn't know exactly what they'd be for, but it sounded good.

He looked at Maria's face, her beautiful eyes locked

into a faraway place of pain where no man could ever go.
"Good Lord, help me," he prayed.

Carol 6: Upon A Midnight Clear

When paramedics Rick Wuerffel and Nick Tranchito arrived at room 313 of the Inn at Bethlehem late on the second-to-last shopping day before Christmas, their jackets were flecked with the blood of a crash victim they'd just helped pry from an overturned SUV on Route 22.

It hadn't been clear, as they'd hopped into their van to obey the dispatcher's urgent instruction to head to the inn, whether the guy in the SUV was going to make it. They left to their colleagues on the squad the job of staving off death in the snow.

Within seconds of turning the knob on 313, it had been clear to the two paramedics that their next task would be helping to bring about birth at the inn.

And that, a few minutes after midnight on Dec. 24, was exactly what they'd done, to the exhausted joy of Maria Encarnacion, 19, new mother, and the hugging, high-fiving gratitude of Jose Carpintero, 20, new father, and Tshaka

Steward, 35, who'd coached the new mother through labor, capping the most amazing day of his 13 years in the hotel business.

Now, Maria's son nestled into the crook of her arm, nosing about for the comfort of wet and warmth. His mother's deep-brown eyes were moist as she kissed his head over and over and over.

"Like a hose, a garden hose," Jose said, wonderingly, to no one in particular.

"What?" Tshaka asked.

"The cord. When the paramedics let me cut the umbilical cord, that's how it felt. Real thick, rubbery."

"I know," said Tshaka, who'd been lost in recollection of the births of his son and daughter. "I remember."

Wuerffel sat down next to Maria with a clipboard and a form. "Excuse me, Mom, a little paperwork." He jotted down her answers. "OK. Father, Jose. Mother, Maria. Time of birth, 12:07 a.m., Dec. 24. Place of birth, Bethlehem."

He studied the sheet, then looked at Maria with a strange smile: "Jose. Maria. Bethlehem. Christmas. Dare I ask what you're naming the little one?"

Maria's face furrowed, then relaxed into a grin: "Oh, no, no, not that. I name him Edgardo, after his grandfather, my father."

"Edgardo it is. Middle name?"

Maria craned her neck gingerly, trying for a better look at Tshaka's blazer, which he'd flung over a chair when he'd begun talking her through contractions.

"Steward. S-T-E-W-A-R-D. Edgardo Steward. My son." Her lips grazed the curly, dark fuzz on his head again.

By 2 a.m., the paramedics had taken mother, son and father to St. Luke's in their van. On the way out, Maria had kissed Tshaka's cheek; Jose had bumped fists with him, saying in a husky voice, "Thanks, bro."

Mel, Gaspar and Baldy, the young couple's three pals who'd been on hand for the drama, snored away in the double room where Tshaka had put them up for the night.

Tshaka walked into his office. His hand ached. Boy, that Maria sure could squeeze when a contraction hit.

To Tshaka's shock, Giles Stone, his boss, who'd come for an inspection visit on the worst night possible, was still there, asleep in a chair. Tshaka had forgotten about him. Stone's head lolled back, mouth agape, a dab of spittle glistening on his lip.

Tshaka tried to slip out noiselessly, but Stone awoke with a start.

"Steward!" he barked.

"It's a boy," Tshaka beamed. "Seven pounds even. 10 on his Apgar. Off to St. Luke's. Mom's fine."

Stone scowled: "That doesn't excuse your lapses in judgment, your lack of control over this property. There will be serious repercussions for this, Steward, serious repercussions."

Tshaka waited out the bluster from Stone, whose hair

was mussed, tie askew, five o'clock shadow deepening. What was it that he felt looking at his boss?

Pity? Yes, pity.

Another feeling gamboled across his brain. Joy. A silvery, twirling joy.

"Merry Christmas, Mr. Stone. Room 446 is made up for you if you need to stay over. I'm going home."

He grabbed his briefcase and turned to the door.

"Steward, I'm not done with you ..." were the last words Tshaka heard.

He walked through the quiet lobby, past the closed doors of the Zinzendorf Room. He loved his hotel at this time of night.

Out on Main Street, the cold stopped his breath. But the snow, the swirling onslaught that had brought chaos to quiet Bethlehem this night, had stopped.

Tshaka looked up, past the streetlights, past the cupola of Central Moravian, past the slumped shadow of South Mountain. Not only had the snow stopped, but a crease had opened in the clouds in the southern sky.

Through it shone the light of a single star.

Tshaka's gloved hand reached up, then flinched, as though expecting to confront a ceiling of glass. But no, his arm stretched full into the crisp air. The star's light seemed to dance upon his fingertip.

What a night it had been. From blizzard to calm. From chaos to miracle. From death on a highway to birth in a hotel. Out of the clouds, a star. Out of the muck of striving, clarity.

Tshaka thought of Maria's lips nuzzling her baby's head. The remembered scent of a newborn sweetly filled his nostrils.

A child is born on this night. On this night, other children wait and dream. Other children. His own.

A calm certainty settled upon Tshaka. He would not be there tomorrow morning, in the cramped office of the Excelsior innkeeper, to parry Giles Stone's rancor. His assistant would be back to handle things. He'd have to dig his car out of the bind his haste had created. Then he'd follow his star, let it guide him back to where he belonged.

He would be in Philadelphia, with his loving children, with their hurt, angry mother. He would express through a Christmas presence his prodigious, prodigal love. He would offer them his better self, as father and husband, not the striving serf he'd too often been.

He would find his way home for Christmas.

"Oh Lord," said Tshaka Steward. "Thank you."

Josh Sees the Light

To Josh Shepard, the blue Saturn out there had the look of a rebel. The endless traffic signal by the KwikFill Mart, where Josh tended the register from 11 p.m. to 7 a.m., drove drivers crazy. Even at 3 a.m., cars just off the ramp from the Blue Route were greeted by a 115-second red, combined with a sadistic no-turn-on-red sign.

That often led to one of two tactics: a defiant turn on red or, from veterans of the corner, a furtive shortcut behind the kiosk where Josh watched nightly over his flock of half-gallons, Marlboro cartons and TastyKakes.

Sure enough, the Saturn inched out on red, and made a dash for it. To keep from imploding with boredom, Josh kept a nightly tally of Shortcutters vs. Red-Busters. So far, the 'Cutters led the Reds 25 nights to 21. In the bonus category of traffic tickets, three of each had been nailed by Officer Harrod, who could get in a foul mood when Josh didn't have a fresh pot of high-test coffee waiting when he stopped in for a courtesy fillup.

It being only three shopping days until Christmas, Josh didn't figure Officer Harrod to be lying in ambush for any innocents tonight.

It was 3:33 a.m. (Josh later recalled he'd glanced at the digital clock on the wall right before it happened.) 'DRE was playing a cut from Alice in Chains' latest CD. Josh had just flipped through Us magazine. (He saved the skin magazines for Monday, as consolation for starting another week as a gas-mart cashier.)

At first, he thought it was just the headlights of a 'Cutter. "Jeez, turn down your brights, buddy," he thought, as an odd glow passed through the store's harsh fluorescence.

But the glow lingered by the south pump island. Josh turned on his stool to look at the idiot who hadn't cut his lights while he pumped unleaded.

There was no car by Pumps 3 and 4.

Instead, a fiercely bright sphere of light, about the size of a healthy grapefruit, hovered, pulsating, a foot above Pump 4.

Adrenaline sluiced through Josh's innards. He felt himself moving, serenely, out the glass door and across the macadam to the pump. The light seemed to be at once right over Pump 4 and tethered to the night firmament, a tunnel of light from the heavens. The light reached out, embraced Josh. "Lord, I'm on X-Files," he thought, calmly, just as the voice began:

"Be not afraid. I bring good news. A child is born, a new chance to a faithless world. Go, Joshua, tell the news: A child is born. Tell the people change can come, for a child is born."

"Whoa!" Josh said. "Huh? What child? Tell who? What's happening?"

"A child is born, Joshua. That is enough to know. Tell the news."

The light pulled away from Josh's face, like a fleeting

caress. "Wait!" he cried, missing its touch. "Who'm I supposed to tell? Wait, you've got to stay and explain . . ." The light was gone.

Josh grabbed Pump 4 to steady himself; he stared a long time at the slot marked "Insert card with black stripe down and to the right."

"Why me?" he thought.

■

It looked more staid than Josh had expected. Instead of a chaos of rattling teletypes and earthy shouts, he gazed across a carpeted warren of cubicles, where dozens of folks stared into computer screens. Still, the sign above the chair where he'd been waiting 30 minutes announced this was the Newsroom.

"The day editor says he's got a free minute."

A clerk gestured Josh to a nearby cubicle. "What do you have for us?" asked Deputy City Editor Thomas Lynch, a husky fellow of about 40 whose hair was making a

Napoleonic retreat from his forehead.

"Look, I don't know how to put this," Josh began slowly, his moist palms rubbing his best, black Dockers. "First thing, I'm not some UFO nut who thinks he's been hosed by aliens. I've got a degree in English — fat load of good it's done me — but anyway, here's the thing: I work at the all-night gas station out where the Blue Route hits the Pike. Last night, something happened there that . . . that's just hard to explain, but it affected me . . . profoundly, you know, and it just seemed real important that I talk to someone with some, you know, power in the media to relay the message."

"Ri-i-i-i-ght," Lynch drawled, flipping through his mental file of methods for blowing off wingnuts gently. "And what might this message be, and from whom?" (Lynch was old-fashioned enough still to care about grammar, fat load of good it was doing his career.)

"A child is born."

"A child is born?"

"Yes, a child is born. Look, I know this sounds like I watch way too much X-Files, but I don't, much anyway, and I swear I was sober. I mean, I was working and my job may suck but I'm not that irresponsible. But anyway, I'm sitting there at 3:33 a.m., precisely, when this, like, cone of light from, you know, up in the sky, focuses like a laser above one of the gas pumps. So, I go check it out, and a voice says — look, I'm not what you think and I wouldn't be here except this experience was so, so compelling — anyway, I hear words coming from inside the light: A child is born. Tell the news. And something about a new chance for a world that doesn't deserve it."

"A second chance, eh?"

"The words just seemed, you know, urgent. A child is

born. It was just so convincing. A child is born."

Lynch decided on Tactic 7, the one for Nice, Harmless Nuts. He swung his computer screen toward Josh.

"Josh . . . that's right, isn't it? Josh, take a gander here. You see this column of words there? Each is what we call a slug, a name for a news story. You know what this one is about? It's about the latest state report on child abuse in this city. You know how many kids were killed by creeps, many of them the creeps that brought them into the world, last year? Seventy-eight. And this piece, here, it's about all the kids at Children's who are crack babies; kids born without a single, stinking chance. We're holding it for a week or so, so we don't depress the hell out of readers until after they sober up from New Year's. Let's see what else . . . a couple of murders, the usual happy tidings from Rwanda.

"Josh, every day we sift through a thousand reports of kids getting born into all kinds of living hell, or being taken out of their lives way too early, and we try to make some sense of it for our readers. Some days we do; some days we don't, but we figure, 'What the hell?' and give folks the bad news anyway. Maybe they can figure it out. It's what we do.

"So, a child is born, you say. A special one. Hooray. And right before Christmas, how 'bout that? Hope he makes a difference, and in 30 years he doesn't get killed like the last one.

"But for now, Josh, I've got a paper to put out about all the nonspecial kids, and all the nonspecial things this ugly world has in store for them. So, Josh, if you'll excuse me …"

"You don't believe me."

"Kid, it ain't my job to believe what can't be proved. Look, either somebody played quite a prank on you, in which case you want the cops, or you saw a miracle, in which case, go talk to a padre. Either way, this isn't the National Enquirer and we aren't interested."

∎

"So, I'm trying to follow what you're telling me, Mr. Shepard," the desk sergeant, a weary, double-shifting mother of two named Elizabeth Pagano said. "You have a report of a missing child, or is it an abandoned baby?" The clammy misery gripped Josh again.

"No, neither exactly. Just an unusual occurrence that ... that might bear investigating, some kind of followup. Maybe a search on one of those police databases?"

"Searching for what, Mr. Shepard? A lost sheep? Sorry, bad joke. I'm kinda punchy."

"I'd like to know if anyone who lives near Blue Route Exit 8 reported any kind of strange atmospheric occurrence, an odd light in the sky, I don't know, strange sounds."

"Oh, a UFO."

"No, no, no, not that."

"Then what?"

Josh sighed. Plunged ahead. "Sergeant, ma'am, I'm not a religious person, really. My parents dragged me to church for years; it never really took though. I don't sit around expecting miracles, you know? But this felt like a miracle, a message from some other place, some other power. It got to me. So if it's just a prank, or a freak of nature, if there's some logic to it, I'd love to know."

Pagano fixed Josh with the look of a mother whose 5-year-old has just learned that, in real life, you sometimes lose at checkers: "Logic, Mr. Shepard? Good Lord, this is no place to come looking for logic, or people with time to find it. This is a nice, quiet suburb, right? Well, in that room back there, the detectives have three unsolved murders on the board, 20 assaults, God knows how many burglaries. Every cruiser we have out today, three days before Christmas, has checked out a call for domestic violence. And you know what the good people of this nice suburb just did last night? They browbeat the pols into cutting the tax rate, which means when three guys on the force retire next year, they won't get replaced. It means no new cars, or guns or body armor. Meanwhile, I work so much OT my Lisa's growing up without a mother.

"You want to know the logic in a light? Good luck. I'm trying to find some logic in the dark.

"Miracles aren't our business, Mr. Shepard. You said you had a church your parents used to drag you to. Well, drag yourself over there. Maybe they're still in the light business."

■

Josh had never before seen the reverend without his robes and collar. But First United's pastor had just put the final touches on the decorations for the Christmas Eve service. So, as the Rev. Dwight Reasoner settled into his leather chair behind his book-laden desk, he wore a red turtleneck, blue jeans and the look of a man at peace in his world: "Josh, excellent to see you. To what do we owe the, may I say, all-too-rare pleasure?"

"Pastor Reasoner, to get right to it, I think I may have witnessed a miracle. I didn't want to believe it, but no other explanation works. Nothing accounts for how changed I feel."

The pastor leaned back in the swivel chair, his fingers in a steeple pressed to his lips: "Mmmm. Go on."

Josh recounted the light over Pump 4, the message, the newspaper, the police station.

With a benign smile, the pastor leaned forward: "Josh, perhaps you'll believe it from me, if not from a cynical newsman or police officer. The age of sky-opening, water-parting miracles is over. It lives for us in our rich and sacred myths, but in rational times, it behooves us to seek deeper understandings. This 'miracle' of yours isn't at all surprising. You're a young man with a questing spirit, aching like all the young for transcendence in a mundane world. For you, this vivid yearning projected itself, as it were, onto the outside world. It speaks well of you, Josh, and it being Christmas week, your subconscious timing was excellent. Your 'light' is calling you back to your community of faith, to a place where the warmth of the people, the beauty of the tradition, can feed you."

"You're saying I was hallucinating?"

"Not in the sense of an LSD flashback or whatever. All I'm saying, Josh, is that the tug of transcendence is resourceful. It will find a way to make itself felt."

"Wow." Josh rose. "I'd have thought a minister would take more interest in a miracle."

"Josh, only a faithless age is in need of signs and miracles. Christian fellowship is already here; it will fill the church tonight just as surely as the choir music, poinsettias and candlelight. Why don't you come? Just sit back and let the feeling wash over you; it will calm you. It will welcome you. It will clarify."

Josh extended his right hand. "Thanks, Reverend. But I'm on duty tonight."

∎

Only 2:59 a.m. Damn! Since the light, nights behind the KwikFill counter had become an agony of clock-watching for Josh. He'd watch the red digits crawl towards 3:33, unable to read, fingers drumming on the cash register, head swiveling to glance at Pump 4 every few seconds. For three nights, he'd waited, heart clamoring, as the right-hand 2 became a third 3. Each night, nothing. No glow, no message, no guidance.

But tonight was Christmas. Tonight had to be different. Fat, moist snowflakes spread a coverlet over Pump 4. Josh straightened the jugs and cartons in the milk case. He glanced at the clock. It was only 3:04.

Then, outside, the rattle of wet gravel, the purr of an engine. Josh peered into the speckled dark. Yow! A stretch limousine, white as the snow, long as a first down. For a long moment, no door opened. Then, unfolding out a rear door, a woman, draped in elegant camel's hair. Words to someone unseen inside, then an oddly familiar toss of glossy, precise hair. She strode across the gathering snow, into recognition.

By the time she was inside, her shaken hair spraying moist jewels of light onto the soft-pretzel case, Josh was speechless. "Excuse me, sir," the woman said. "May I ask a question that may seem, well, a bit odd?"

"Y-y-ou're . . ." Josh managed one word.

The woman's sigh mixed pleasure and resignation, as she peered at his nametag: "Yes, Josh, Oprah Winfrey. Pleased to meet you."

After the handshake: "And you're wondering what I'm doing outside Philadelphia on Christmas Eve, or Day, whatever it is, instead of roasting chestnuts in Chicago, right?"

Josh smiled serenely: "The light, right?"

Oprah Winfrey clutched his right hand in both of hers: "My God, this is the place. I thought so, but Ann didn't. We've been wandering for hours in that limo, worried we'd lost our marbles, wondering what the tabs would do with us once they found out. But you've had the dream? About the light, the muffled message you can't quite hear?"

"Uh, no, Ms. Winfrey," Josh said, then hurried on as her gleaming smile evaporated. "I mean, it was no dream.

It was real. The light was here three nights ago, right there over Pump 4. I went to it and it surrounded me and I heard the message quite clearly. It said . . ."

"Wait!" her ribbon-red nails rose imperiously before Josh's face. "Don't tell me yet. I must get the others." She clicked out to the limo, peered in, and was soon joined by two other women, older, one lean and regal, the other gnomish, comical.

Holding each other's elbows, they slushed back to the kiosk. Entering, they blinked in the unsparing light.

"That's him," Oprah said excitedly. "He knows. He really saw it. Here!"

"Well, call me Amazed in Philadelphia," the taller woman said, chuckling. "It seems in the excitement my dear friend Oprah has neglected her manners. I'm delighted to meet you, Mr. . . . ?"

"Shepard, Josh Shepard." Neurons buzzed about Josh's brain, trying to place the new faces.

"Shepard? My goodness, this is getting eerie. Oh, but I forget my manners, too. Josh, I'm Ann Landers."

"And am I just a plate of gelfite fish, zot no one thinks to mention?" the little woman said in mock dismay. "Josh, R-r-ruth Westheimer. Goot to know you." She shook his hand, then nudged her companions: "Oooh, vot lovely muscles in zuh arm, zis boy."

The neurons clicked into place. "Dr. Ruth! Of course! I used to listen to you when I was 13 and, well, never mind. And, Ms. Landers, my mom reads you every day, and, Ms. Winfrey, she watches you. But, how . . ."

"In the world did we get here? That's a tale, honey, a tale," Oprah chuckled. "Where to start, ladies? Well, 11 days ago I started having this vivid dream. I was walking toward a light, in the snow, at some deserted gas station, and somebody was saying something I couldn't quite hear, and I'd look left to ask the person next to me if they could make it out, and it was always Ann."

"So," the famed counselor picked up the thread, "the dream so troubled Oprah she finally rang me at my place in Chicago. I told her I was having the same dream, nearly, except I looked to my left and saw . . . "

"Me!" Dr. Ruth emitted a triumphant giggle. "Und me? I'd been having zuh same dream, very arousing, but with both zese two in it. Imagine! When zey called and told me, I rushed to Chicago like it vass a session with zat Alec Baldvin."

"Yesterday, we spent driving about Chicago aimlessly, looking for the gas station," Ann Landers said. "Then Oprah just looked at us and said, 'Philadelphia,' and we said, 'Yes, that's right.' We flew here in her jet this evening. We drove for hours until we came here."

"Oy, and a cold comingk ve had of it, too," Dr. Ruth moaned. "Oprah, you von't believe me, but I tell you, zot heater does not work."

"And now, we've arrived here, to meet the fascinatingly named Josh," Ann Landers said. Oprah looked at her quizzically.

"Make the connection, Oprah, dear. Josh Shepard. Shep-herd. Waiting and watching by night. Which, on Christmas Eve, makes us . . ."

"The Three Wise Women," Josh completed, matter of fact. "The Magi."

"Ze Magpies, you mean," Dr. Ruth blurted, cracking herself up.

"So, what now, Josh? What now? I've never felt less like a wise woman," Oprah said. "What are we doing here exactly, except giving the National Enquirer a photo-op to die for? Oh, we never did get back to what that message was. What was it, anyway?"

"Be not afraid. I bring good news. A child is born, a second chance to a faithless world. Go and tell the news: A child is born. Tell the people change can come, for a child is born."

"My gootness, vot am I doing-k here, me a Jew?" Dr. Ruth asked.

"Or me? Call me Stupefied in Suburbia."

"Never before have I been so scared to ask the next question," Oprah said. "Josh, why are we here?"

"I stewed about this for days, and got nowhere," Josh said. "Then, when your limo pulled up, somehow down here" — he tapped his heart — "I knew. Now, the news has made its way up here." He thunked his temple.

"Tell it, oh, Shepard." Ann Landers' eyes were merry.

"Dr. Ruth, don't worry. I don't think you've been dragged to a Second Coming, or a First, I guess, in your case." Josh's tone was firm. "In the last few days, I've seen people who think they care, who want to care, but can't remember how. It's been beaten or smoothed out of them. I think 'A child is born' just means that every second God sends us a new reason to care, to change. If we could only stop, just a moment, to look, really look, at one newborn child, and think, really think, what we owe it, what world we ought to leave it, instead of the one we will, that might make us change. Yes, that's it. Once you've really looked at a child, the way the light shows the child, you will be changed."

"I need that," Oprah said quietly.

"But," Josh held her hands tightly, scanned three sets of staring eyes, "if you go to the light, to be within it, there's no going back. Things just won't be the same. You won't be the same. You can't . . . Oh, God!"

"What?" the three cried.

"It's almost 3:33," Josh said, a finger poised in the air, then falling: "Now."

The glow filled the kiosk, rich and playful. Four heads leaned into it, eyes searching Pump 4 through the swirling snow. One second, nothing hovered above it; dread squeezed Josh's stomach. The next, the light was there, arcing to the firmament.

"What now, Josh?" Oprah murmured.

"If you can bear to change, you go to the light."

"Change is goot." Dr. Ruth bustled to the door.

"Wait, Ruth," Ann Landers said. "We have no gifts. What kind of magpies, uh, Magi, are we?"

Oprah reached into her bag. "I have one of my autographed mugs." And Ann Landers into hers: "I'll autograph my column from this morning's paper."

"Und I just hoppen to have a zigned copy of my new

book!" Dr. Ruth said.

"Shall we go, ladies?" Josh asked, jauntily crooking his arms.

"Lead on, young Shepard," Ann Lander said, taking an arm. "You go, girl," Oprah said, taking another.

"Oy, you leave an old lady nothing to grab," Dr. Ruth said, beaming. "Zo, fine. I lead."

She opened the door, stepped into the moist, glowing snow; the others followed.

Slowly, like toddlers creeping to their parents' room at dawn, they moved toward Pump 4, toward the fierce, caressing light.

The Nick of Time

A Hard Landing

The chopper landed in the maw of a blizzard. Once Blunt was out and clear of the spinning rotors, they stripped off his blindfold. He fell to his knees in the deep snow, staggered by the abrupt change from noisy blackness to stinging whiteout.

"Pah, every Thanksgiving weekend, we get one of

these," Phineas grumbled into Blunt's ear. "Best wait until the wind dies a tad. No point stumbling off in the wrong direction."

"Phineas!" Blunt's voice braided fear and anger. "What the hell is going on? Where are we?"

"Patience, lad, it'll soon be clear."

After five minutes, the blizzard relented.

"Hurry along," Phineas said, gripping Blunt's elbow with a sinewy strength. "We're late and this blockhead of a pilot has put us down a fair stroll from base. We'd best not test the Boss' patience, thin as it's been."

Blunt struggled to keep pace with the brisk little figure. He peered through the snowy twilight.

In 20 years as a journalist, Blunt had witnessed some vivid sights: the eye of a hurricane from a weather plane, St. Patrick's packed and hushed for a Kennedy funeral, the midnight frenzy at the end of a legislative session, as pols roar and scowl.

This vista topped them all. In the middle distance, a cluster of white domes rose — a huge central one, 10 stories high, smaller mounds huddled around it. Each dome was circled by bands of green and red, and topped with banners of the same hues, snapping in the Arctic wind.

A door slid open in one dome. A shaft of light, golden, playful, leaped into the stubborn dusk. Blunt stopped, exhaling with a whistle.

Phineas grinned: "Quite the show, eh? They all stop to drink it in about here. But best keep moving."

Pressing forward with surer strides, Blunt murmured: "I'll be damned. I'm on the roof of the world, at the doorstep of legend."

Then a stab of panic: The miniature video camera! Did he have it? Blunt patted his parka.

Phineas was at his elbow again: "Pahh, Mr. Blunt. You did not lose it. We took it, while you were sleeping on the flight up. Once you're done here, you'll get it back. Thought we were silly geese, did you? We've been dealing with the clever likes of you for ages, we have. Rules are rules, Mr. Blunt. No recording devices! Just a pencil and pad, and we'll provide those, thank you very much.

"Now," Phineas tugged Blunt toward the opening, "let's get inside. There's a form or two for you to sign before you can see the Boss."

They crossed the threshold; the door slid closed behind, banishing the ice and gloom to another universe. They were in an entrance hall: warm wood, bright sconces, fragrant evergreens. At the far end, a thick wood door cracked open just enough to hint at bustle beyond.

Phineas stamped some snow off the curled toes of his boots.

"Welcome, Mr. Blunt," the old elf said, bowing so low his sharp nose nearly scraped the stone floor, "to the North Pole. Welcome to the home of his eminence, Santa Claus."

The Truth About Clarence

Blunt was getting writer's cramp from signing the elf's "form or two."

A waiver of frostbite liability . . . a release to treat him, if necessary, for reindeer tick fever . . . permission to use his photo in Workshop Wanderings, the in-house newsletter.

"I had no idea the North Pole was so bureaucratic," Blunt whined.

"Truly, lad, you have no idea," Phineas replied, thrusting another paper across his desk, on which a nameplate announced: Phineas T. Galadriel, Chief Executive Elf. "This would be the last of them."

Blunt glanced at it: "Oath of Non-disclosure? What the devil!?" His hazel eyes scanned the form.

"Is this some kind of joke?" Blunt sputtered at Phineas, who gazed back serenely. "You lure me with promises of an exclusive interview with a reclusive celebrity who admires my work. You wave off my natural questions, set all kinds of bizarre conditions. But I figure, what the heck, I can spare a few days for a lark. You drag me on an eight-hour flight, then a blindfolded chopper ride where I was sure death was my copilot. You steal my camera. Finally, I figure out I'm at the North Pole and the hook is that Santa Claus really exists. And, hey, I'm fine with that. Then you tell me with your whiskery face hanging out that I can't WRITE ABOUT IT?!?! Are you nuts? I'm a journalist; I'm writing about this, pal."

"If that is your position," Phineas said, an elfin hint of a smile on his lips, "then we shall blindfold you in a trice and take you back to your office in Philadelphia. You would forgo seeing how we manage the complex choreography of Christmas Eve, would not see the Santa clone farm, would not feed Blitzen a carrot. You would not, most assuredly, meet the Boss. It is, of course, your choice."

"This is outrag- . . . Wait, did you say clone farm?"

"Yes. 'Twas a favorite stop among your predecessors, all of whom, I might add, signed that form — yet managed to use what they learned here quite profitably."

"My predecessors?"

"Yes, Mr. Blunt. As you would know if you had read carefully, instead of blustering away, you are not forbidden to write about the North Pole. You are merely forbidden to represent what you write as fact."

"Which is what I do for a living," Blunt muttered.

"Yes, yes, Mr. Blunt, but use some imagination. Clement Moore did, Francis Church did. Mr. Dickens, bless his soul, surely did. These are names you recognize, I imagine?"

"Dickens, sure. Moore, that's the 'Night before Christmas' guy, right? The other one is . . . ?"

"The New York Sun editorialist who penned the words, 'Yes, Virginia, there is a Santa Claus,' words whose lasting fame no doubt stems from their having been based on journalistic certitude."

"They all came here?"

"Yes. The Boss has long been an avid reader and art connoisseur. His visiting artists program is in its 195th year. Writers, artists, and in this century, filmmakers."

"Unbelievable! Like who?"

"Mr. Frank Capra, for example, whom my very own Uncle Clarence, bless his bumbling soul, escorted about. And the fellow who wrote that Tim Allen movie, though we had a bit of a dustup because his script edged a little too close to the truth. Some fellows don't write a thing, but still benefit. Take Salman Rushdie; he visited, liked it, stayed six months. Said it was as good a hiding place as any.

"But," Phineas rose, scooping up the papers, "since our little oath so offends your journalistic honor, I shall tell The Boss his choice this year declined. Just as well, really."

"Not so fast," Blunt grabbed the elf's arm. "Maybe this'll work. Details might go for a mock interview, kinda postmodern. And they pay good."

"Very well, then," the elf sighed. "On to the clone farm."

Blunt rose to follow Phineas out, then paused: "One more question: Why me?"

"That is simple," Phineas said, turning with a hand on the doorknob. "You were the only syndicated columnist in America this year not to put the name Monica Lewinsky in your pieces even once. You, Thomas Blunt, have been a very good boy."

The wonders of the North Pole

Blunt hunched forward on a chair in the bustling anteroom to Santa Claus' office. His interview was to start in 10 minutes.

He flipped through a notepad where he'd recorded dazzled observations of the North Pole tour he'd taken

A CHRISTMAS QUARTET 63

with Phineas, the head elf.

In this labyrinth beneath a cluster of domes on the Arctic surface, new wonders arose at every turn. Blunt read over notes jotted in his spidery scrawl:

Microsoft meets Kris Kringle. No quaint woodworkers' shop this. Monitors, computers, electronics everywhere. The elves — beards, yes, but Dockers and flannel shirts, not little green felt outfits. Short, but not tiny — wiry, STRONG. Friendly, but focused on work. Nothing but high praise for The Boss: genius, generous, jokester, blah, blah, blah. But several ask P., "How's The Boss doing today?" Furrowed brows. What's up?

First stop: NON Central. NON for "Naughty or Nice." The heart of Santa's global behavior monitoring system. Have yourself a CIA little Christmas. Huge room. Banks upon banks of monitors. Elves at control panels, headphones on, switching from image to image on screens, scribbling notes. P. sez: Guy who wrote The Truman Show was here two years back.

At NON Central, video from all corners of the globe

had danced across the screens. Elves listened in on a babble of conversations: English, Spanish, Latvian, Farsi, Bantu.

Phineas had explained the system. On some screens, the video was live, patched in from surveillance cameras operating around the world: in classrooms, public squares, Dunkin Donuts. Some of it was tape sent in by thousands of "watcher elves," who monitored children in person.

"Not hardly," Phineas had chuckled when Blunt asked whether every child in the world was monitored. "We're not God, you know. First, we weed out those who don't believe in Christmas. After that, all we can manage is a computer-generated random sample each year; a lad's chance of being 'on tab,' as we call it, is about one in a million. Now, mind you, NON Central may run around the clock, but any one lad or lass is watched only a few minutes a day. For their sake, you hope those are well-behaved minutes."

"Just minutes? Is that fair?" Blunt had asked.

"Is life?" Phineas had shrugged. "We tinker to add fairness. Lately, we've tried some newfangled theory called benchmarking, grading each child against the median behavior for his Myers-Briggs personality type. Some call it progress, Mr. Blunt; others call it pish-posh. We had quite the nurture vs. nature debate in the Elves Council before we passed that idea up to The Boss."

The Eve Room. The Pole's nerve center — Blunt's notes went on — *The logistics of Christmas night get game-planned, reviewed and revised year-round. year-round. Sign says: Failure Is Not an Option. Route maps, full of zigs and zags, flash on a wall screen. Elves gesture, argue, pound at keyboards. "The old man can't handle it," one says. "Never seen the tangle he couldn't untangle," another replies.*

"We don't go to every house," Phineas had explained. "Used to, back in the 1800s. Can't come close now, with the way this thing has grown. Now, that Naughty-Nice Median is our guide. The more a lad strays from it, for good or ill, the more likely we'll be visiting. No coal in stockings anymore, though. We've got our environmental lobby, too. But we have our ways. Mind, some work gets done before the big night. A good lass' parents might go to Toys R Us and find one more of a supposedly out-of-stock doll. A naughty lad, his folks might just happen to buy the one box that's missing assembly instructions."

The Santa Clone Farm. Eerie — the word was underlined three times on the notepad — A hall hundreds of yards long. Thick, clear cylinders, triple-stacked, covered in frost. Many dials, wires. In each, a plump, bearded fellow in a red suit, asleep, smiling. Clones! Cryogenics!

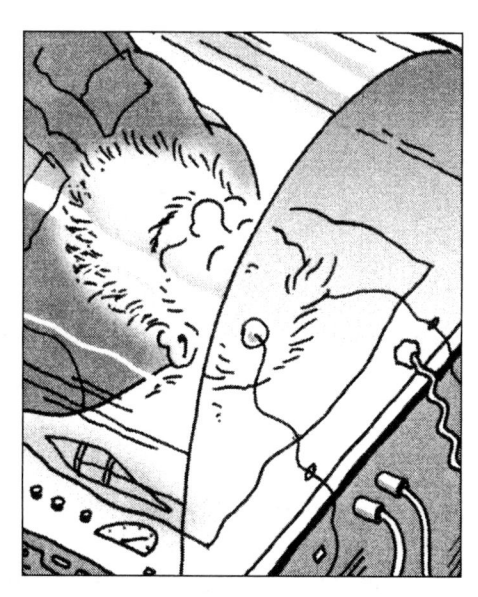

"We had the secret to cloning for, oh, a century before we used it," Phineas had explained. "The Boss has connections, of course. But he was reluctant to accept the help, he was. The classic Type A, our Boss. Finally, after our tongues were all dragging from the workload, he had to face facts. He put very strict rules on it, though. We don't unfreeze the lads here until a week before the big day. A few tests, some drills, and they're good to go. But Dec. 26, it's back in the tubes. Poor buggers."

Where are the toys? P. sez: Santa mostly contracts that out now. Master elves make a few select items that Santa himself designs. These go to the good kids Santa personally delivers to. He picks them from printouts done by NON Central.

Blunt reached the end of his notes. His mind raced: "Best stuff I ever got in my career, but how can I use it? What am I gonna do?"

A shadow fell upon his hunched form. He looked up. It was Holly, The Boss' secretary: "Mr. Blunt, he'll see you now."

A Little Time with Nick

"Right this way, Mr. Blunt."

As Blunt's feet took him across the threshold of legend, Holly the secretary shut the door behind him.

The room was dim. His eyes roved, hungry for details. His heart quickened. When was the last interview that had done that?

"Ah, Mr. Blunt, come in," a voice crept over the back of a large wooden rocker across the oval room.

Blunt walked toward the voice, noting the simple furnishings: the rocker, a Shaker table and chairs, one bookcase, one wall hanging of a red cross on green background. Austere, a monk's cell.

The rocker turned on the bare stone floor. Blunt beheld Santa Claus.

The girth, the beard, the gold-rimmed glasses all confirmed myth. No red suit, though; flannels and a bulky cardigan. And the eyes peering at Blunt conveyed not mirth, but weariness.

Santa rose with a wan smile: "Mr. Blunt, welcome. I am Nicholas of Myra. Ah, don't be puzzled. I am a man of many nicknames: Sinter Claes, Pere Noel, Father Christmas, Kris Kringle. But the man I was born long ago I remain: Nicholas, God's servant from Myra. Called by others a saint, but knowing himself a sinner. Please, sit."

Blunt sat, fumbled for his notepad and pencil, could not manage speech.

"I trust the good Phineas kept you amused visiting the various nooks of our little domain."

"Uh, yes, Sa — . . . er, Nicholas. Remarkable, dazzling." Blunt recovered his journalistic footing: "I was surprised to see how much energy goes into logistics, how little into making toys."

St. Nicholas sighed. He removed his spectacles, rubbed his eyes for a long while, then spoke: "So true, Mr. Blunt. We started here centuries ago, Phineas' ancestors and I, working with our hands, with wood, with straw, with homespun cloths, making dolls, tops, simple playthings to delight the innocent mind.

"Now" — he replaced his glasses on his nose — "I sit atop a global, high-tech enterprise. Making a toy by hand, talking to a child — ah, those are now all-too-rare pleasures."

"How do you spend your days, then?"

"How else does a modern CEO spend his days, Mr. Blunt?" The saint managed a wry smile. "In meetings. Poring over printouts. In negotiations. Do you know there are seven unions among the elves of the North Pole? All with contracts that expire Nov. 15. No contract, no

Christmas. Unions are an instrument of justice, I know, but sometimes, Mr. Blunt, justice is a bear."

Blunt began to laugh, but a look at St. Nicholas' eyes cut him short. The bearded man resumed:

"There is so much to keep one's eye on, a thousand streams of detail and care all flowing toward one goal, one night. Struggling to make fair judgments on the children. Cataloging their wishes. Managing the contractors who make the bulk of the toys, avoiding sweatshops and child labor. Trying to keep costs in line. These Nintendo games, Mr. Blunt! Do you know what an ill-timed blip in the cost of microchips can do to my budget?"

"Forgive me, but you don't sound much like Jolly St. Nick."

The whiskery face winced.

"Mr. Blunt, I was . . . I am a man of God. Long ago, I was a bishop. When my time came to leave this world, the Lord came to me. He spoke of the special joy I found in giving to children. He proposed to me a special ministry, using my joy to teach, to heal. I agreed and received this, this . . . not immortality, but vast extension of old age.

"Ahhh, it's been wonderful, mostly. A child's cry of delight, the joyous flutter of an innocent soul — to see those so often, it's been more than this old sinner deserved. But, of late, this century, my role has grown too large. Not just the number of children. Their expectations, their lust for ... for things. I'm not capable of ignoring the wish of a child, but sometimes these modern children want so much . . . too much. Half of the time, I fret that I can't do enough for them; the rest of the time I worry that I do far too much.

"My job, Mr. Blunt, is to bear witness to the good, to hold up the loving joy of giving. But look at this grand machine for the transport and delivery of things I have built here under the ice. Then tell me: Have I gotten it all backwards? Do I feed the evil fire of materialism in this soul-sick world, not the pure fire of love?"

A wintry smile.

"Listen to an old man who's lived too long, Mr. Blunt. It is a high calling to meet the needs of others; but it is a hard ending to become a prisoner of their expectations."

He patted his belly, tried a warmer smile. "Do you know that when Thomas Nast visited here, I had a 34-inch waist? But he drew an extra 50 pounds on me, and I've been growing into his expectations ever since. It seems I can't help doing that."

Blunt's mind whirred but couldn't find a sensible question. His eye fell on the screensaver on the saint's computer: a famous painting in a lush tropical palette of deep greens and earthy browns.

"Is that a Gauguin there?"

St. Nicholas glanced at the image: "Marvelous painter, so primal, so bold. In life, too. I sometimes think he had the right idea.... Well, Mr. Blunt, sorry to cut this short, but in this season there is so much to do. Perhaps we can chat again."

Blunt stumbled from the gloomy room, welcoming the bright bustle beyond the door.

Tears of a Clone

Blunt's gloomy interview with St. Nicholas having ended, he was escorted by a young elf back to Phineas Galadriel's office.

"Well, then," Phineas said, looking up from a stack of printouts. "How did your little chat go?"

Blunt hesitated: "Morosely. Are you sure the Boss doesn't suffer from seasonal affective disorder or something?"

"Hmmmm... well, 'tis the season to be stressed, as the saying goes up here." A chuckle died in Phineas' throat. "There's a sight more to making Christmas happen than ho-ho-ho, and it feels a burden to him sometimes, I'm sure. Very much so lately, it seems."

Phineas stared into space a moment, then slapped his desktop.

"Tell you what, Mr. Blunt. Come the morrow, the Boss makes his annual trip to Macy's in New York, he does. Stands in for the stand-ins, so to speak. Gets to dandle many a child on his knee, chat with 'em. Always perks him right up. Stay over with us, and I'll get you back in to see him in two days' time."

So Blunt did. There was plenty to keep him intrigued the next day: the reindeer training barn, the toy design lab, the Itchy Dwarf (the elves' noisy off-hours hangout).

At 9 a.m. sharp the following day, Holly ushered Blunt back into the Boss' spartan sanctuary.

The saint, clad this time in traditional red, indeed seemed transformed, his cheeks pink, his eyes merry, his voice a hearty rumble.

"Ho-ho-ho!" he roared. "And who might you be?"

"Thomas Blunt, sir. The visiting writer? We spoke day

before last?"

"Well, sure, sure. But call me Santa, son. And how might I make you merry? Ho-ho-ho!"

Blunt stared at the chortling man. Was this some practical joke? Where was the troubled saint of two days before?

"I wanted to ask some follow-up questions to our talk."

"Well, fine, fine, fine. Ho-ho-ho. And what can I get ye for Christmas?"

It was like a corny tape playing inside the red suit; the gestures were jerky, overdrawn.

Blunt clicked his tongue against clenched teeth, nodded curtly, turned on his heel, stormed down the hall to Phineas' office.

"What's the big idea, Phineas?" Blunt glowered at the elf across the low tabletop. "Keep me cooling my heels for two days, then pawn me off on some cheap Santa clone!"

"What foolishness are you babbling, lad?"

"That clown in the office down the hall is a clone, not

the real Nicholas, that's what."

"Impossible, Mr. Blunt. By law, it's two weeks yet until the clones can be unfrozen, and only The Boss has the codes."

Phineas stared at Blunt. Blunt stared at Phineas. "Oh . . . my . . . Lord," the elf whispered.

"What, Phineas, what?"

Without a word, Phineas swept from the room, Blunt trailing.

"Hello, Boss," Phineas was saying by the time Blunt, panting, reached the doorway of St. Nicholas' office. "Had a chance to review the Central American TripTik yet?"

"Come again, little fella? Ho-ho-ho!" Santa's eyes darted about.

"Excuse me, Boss," Phineas said, edging toward the desk. "You've got a feather or something on the collar of your suit."

The elf hopped nimbly onto the desk, grabbed the collar behind the neck, then tugged sharply down. A silver chain became visible along the base of the neck. Phineas yanked at the chain, rotating it until he grasped a dog tag in his thin hands.

Santa looked quizzically at Blunt.

"Holy eggnog and mistletoe," Phineas murmured.

"What is it, Phineas?" Blunt gazed at the engraved dog tag.

"This is not the Boss. This is Clone No. 63453."

"Then where is St. Nicholas?"

"I . . . have . . . no . . . idea."

Olivetti and Eureka

Phineas shoved Blunt into his office, locked the door

and paced about, running thin fingers through wiry hair. Then he stood arms akimbo, tongue out, the curled-toe boot on his left foot tapping.

Back in St. Nicholas' office, Santa Clone No. 63453 sat gagged and bound to the rocker. Phineas had told Holly that the Boss wasn't feeling well. Hold all calls and visitors.

Phineas winced: "Mr. Blunt, my friend, I must ask you to do what won't come naturally to a journalist. We must keep this a secret until I can decide what to do. We must avoid a panic."

A protest flared in Blunt's brain, then died. He'd come to like this crafty elf. He smiled: "Relax, Phineas, it's not like I can dial the City Desk from here and yell, 'Sweetheart, get me rewrite.'"

"Just so, Mr. Blunt, just so. Thank you for your discretion. The stakes are indeed high. Nothing less than Christmas morning for millions of lads and lasses."

Blunt snorted: "Just a little dramatic, aren't we, Phineas? Seems to me this high-tech machine at the North Pole pretty much runs itself, and what it needs you give it. The Boss seems more like the Figurehead, if you ask me. A pretty mopey one, too."

Phineas' eyes flashed: "Watch your tongue, lad. You've no idea what you're saying. All that you've seen here, the

Eve Room, NON Central, the clones — it's all an extension of the Boss' will, his genius, his goodness. Without him, we are lost. We can make toys and plot routes until the caribou come home. But it is St. Nicholas of Myra, none other, who provides the sparks of inspiration that make every Christmas special."

Phineas fixed Blunt with a sly look: "Yes, sparks of inspiration. Like that Olivetti of yours."

Blunt's stomach flipped: "The Olivetti? You mean — ?"

"Yes, lad," Phineas said. "Begging your pardon, but did you really think that sad, alcoholic father of yours had the wit to buy such a present for you in the Christmas of '63?"

The fake tree listed wearily next to the radiator in the shabby Blunt apartment. A few plain ornaments and crinkled strands of tinsel hung on the lower boughs where young Thomas had hung them the night before as his parents dozed, drinks in hand. A few awkwardly wrapped presents were scattered beneath the tree — and one large, mysterious, perfect box. At 9 o'clock Christmas morn, after Thomas had dragged his bleary parents from bed, he raced for that box. Ripping it open, he pulled out a small Olivetti typewriter, banged excitedly on the keys. "Phil, you fool," Thomas' mother

rasped, *"how could you spend all that without telling me?" "Don't look at me,"* he replied.

"That afternoon, I watched a football game on TV," Blunt said to Phineas, dreamily. "Took notes on that typewriter, then wrote up a game story. Pretty soon, I was writing up whole imaginary newspapers for imaginary towns.

"From that Christmas on, I knew what I wanted to be. I was hooked. That gift changed my life."

"Of course it did, Thomas," Phineas said. "That's how The Boss planned it. That's the kind of thing he, and only he, can do every Christmas for thousands of little ones."

"Well, we've got to find him." Blunt was fervent.

"Yes, yes, but how? I knew he was a bit wearier than usual this season, but I had no idea he'd do this. Probably he sent the clone on the Macy's jaunt yesterday; it's the kind of rote day a clone could handle. That means he has two days' jump on us. He could be anywhere; after all, he knows his way around the planet better than anyone. And there's only the two of us, you and me, who must find him. We don't dare tell anyone else, so close to Christmas. There'd be a panic."

Phineas sighed: "You know, Mr. Blunt, all the elves I came up with have retired by now. Big, fat pensions and all day for golf. At times like these I think maybe they had the right idea."

Blunt's head popped up: "Wait, Phineas, what did you say?"

"I said, at times like these I think those elves had the right idea. What of it, lad?"

"Phineas, call in the chopper! I know where he is!"

"Where? What? What d'you mean, lad? You look all wild!"

"Just get the darn chopper revving, my friend. There'll

be plenty of time in the air to explain."

Good Nick Hunting

As the chopper rose, the clustered domes of St. Nicholas' North Pole domain receded, blending into the white vastness.

Blunt yelled to Phineas over the thumping of the rotors: "You're sure the plane will be waiting in Greenland?"

"Yes, yes, Mr. Blunt. Really, now that you've got me up here, ordering planes at your command, you must let me in on this hunch of yours."

"Tahiti, Phineas, Tahiti."

"Whatever do you mean? Tahiti is on the other side of the globe."

"Precisely its appeal to a burned-out, depressed CEO. Ever notice that St. Nicholas' computer has a Gauguin screensaver?"

"Gauguin? My word, I hadn't noticed that. But what of it?"

"When I commented on it, The Boss said the same thing about Gauguin that you said back there about an elf who took early retirement: 'Sometimes I think he had the right idea.' And what did Gauguin do? Throw in his whole life in France and run off to Tahiti. Elementary, my dear Phineas."

"Indeed, Mr. Blunt, indeed." The elf exhaled, then grinned, "Well, then, the game is afoot."

■

A long, hot coming they had of it, did Thomas Blunt and Phineas Galadriel. For anyone, the North Pole to Tahiti would be a drastic adjustment in time and temperature.

For bodies who raced from the Pole in parkas without a thought to packing, the last legs of the long trip were a sweaty affair. Damp and bedraggled, the lanky Blunt and elfin Phineas drew stares as they stumbled into the first island shop they saw in Tahiti and scarfed up T-shirts and shorts.

"Phineas, I'd say you looked sporty, if those shorts weren't three sizes too big," Blunt joshed at the taxi stand.

"By a polar bear's tail, how does anyone survive in this blasted sun?" Phineas gasped, licking sweat with his tongue.

In the taxi, Blunt turned to Phineas: "No way to ask this delicately, but does The Boss have . . . well, an eye for the ladies?"

"There is no Mrs. Claus, you know. That's a fancy of your Madison Avenue. The Boss was a bishop, you recall. But though he's a saint, he is a man. And looking, he always says, is not a sin. Your point?"

"Take us to the beachfront hotels, cabbie," was Blunt's reply.

At curbside in front of a row of hotels, the two split up, agreeing to meet in an hour. Blunt read the sign in front of one hotel: *Visit Gauguin's Hideaway. Happy hour 4-6.*

Bingo, he thought.

Blunt wended his way through the lobby to a poolside, open-air bar with an angled, thatched roof. He spied a large, bearded form in a tropical shirt and straw hat, hunched over the bar, idly stirring the umbrella in his fruity drink.

Blunt sidled out into the sunshine, working his way around a line of chaises packed with shapely suntans. From five feet behind, he gazed sympathetically at the sagging bulk. Then he said heartily: "St. Nicholas!"

The shoulders flinched. After a long pause, the old man set down his drink and turned on the stool.

"Mr. Blunt." A tiny smile. "I should have known to wait until the investigative journalist left the premises."

"Nicholas, come back."

"Too late. It is too late and I am too little, my boy. I am used up. Not even the South Sea sun that fired Gauguin's imagination can raise the tiniest spark in me."

"Because this is not your world, your mission, Nicholas. They await you far from here."

"Ha! Why, Mr. Blunt? So I can help choke the world a bit more with the glittering, chilling things it lusts after? It long ago got away from me, my mission, and I can't get it back."

"Ridiculous. This world needs Santa Claus more than ever."

"My dear Mr. Blunt, there is no Santa Claus."

'No, Nicholas, there is a Santa Claus. And you are he. You are the one who in 1963 gave a lonely little boy a strange gift, an Olivetti typewriter, that deflected his dark life into the light, gave him purpose, joy and passion. Now it's time to give the same back to the giver. That boy is standing in front of you, Nicholas, as he probably was fated to do from the moment he opened that box.

"They all have purpose, these gifts you bring, these little joys you sow around the globe on Christmas morning. They remind a faithless age that there is hope, a selfish age that there is joy in generosity. They stun the sour with serendipity, surprise the cynical with random kindness. They teach the children that, despite the mounting evidence of their eyes, life sometimes does reward virtue, shun evil. They are a tangible spark of the divine, pointing anyone with a lick of sense to the larger mystery of the day.

"And only you, Nicholas of Myra, have the gift of giving such gifts. There is a Santa Claus, whose mission greed and ego cannot shackle. And you are he, Nicholas of Myra, and no other."

Blunt reached a hand toward the old man, who was staring at him as though he were a ghost: "Come, let's go home."

Nicholas' eyes locked on Blunt's for a long moment. Then it began, with a shudder of Nicholas' shoulders, which spread to his arms. By the time it reached his belly, it had become a shake, then it rumbled up through his chest into his throat and to his lips. Out those lips it came: *HO-HO-HO-HO-HO!*, a rich laugh that flew around the bar, turning heads and making smiles, then danced right up Nicholas' nose into his eyes.

Their mirth overflowed as tears. Nicholas shook and laughed, removed his glasses, wiped his eyes.

With a chuckle and a sigh, Nicholas looked Blunt again in the eye.

"What?" Blunt asked

Then it all began again, the shoulder shudder and belly shake and the rumbling laugh, until folks around the bar were laughing along with the big man with the white beard, though they had no idea why. *HO-HO-HO-HO-HO!* Nicholas laughed until his breath gave out.

"What?" Blunt, the only person in the bar not chortling, asked again. "What is so funny?"

"Well, my eloquent friend," Nicholas said. "I looked at you and it occurred to me it had taken a reporter to restore my idealism. That most perfect of cynics, a reporter!"

"Well," Blunt said, grinning. "We're not totally worthless, then."

"No indeed, Thomas, no indeed." Nicholas hopped off

the barstool and threw his arm around Blunt.

"Phineas came with you? Yes? Then let's gather him up before he gets into trouble and hustle ourselves back to the Pole.

"Santa Claus has a Christmas to run!"

A Christmas Carol @mega-ware.com

Disk 1: Simon's Ghost

Quentin Stiles was rich. There was no doubt whatsoever about that.

The debate was whether he was (as Forbes magazine claimed) not only the richest man alive, but also the Richest Man in the History of the World. Stiles rather suspected he'd earned the title. But what he fancied more was recognition as the smartest man in the world. Wealth was just a way to keep score.

On this gloomy December day — not that gloom could penetrate the high-tech cocoon (its lighting, heat, humidity and 20-speaker sound system all calibrated to his precise whim) where Stiles reigned at Mega-ware Inc.'s Denver headquarters — the Richest Man in the History of the World was annoyed.

Mightily annoyed. Fingers thrumming on his ergonomic keyboard, eyes glaring at his ultra-high resolution screen, he spat out a single word:

"Idiot."

How, he thought, can a brain I pay so well to write programming code better than anyone else at Mega-ware be so dim?

■

Poor Blodgett. A few minutes ago, when he'd clicked *Send* on the e-mail that now glowed meekly on Stiles' screen, he'd felt a silvery joy.

In a sleepless burst of code-writing fever, he'd done it. He, Dan Blodgett, had sliced the binary knot that had slowed progress on Thresholds 99, the latest update of Mega-ware's colossally dominant operating system for personal computers. As tangled and twisted as the path there had been, that's how crisp, elegant, and full of light his solution now seemed. Surely Quentin would be pleased, he thought. No more fretting that his team wouldn't have Thresholds 99 ready for beta testing in January, or ready for its rollout by April in the boxes with the royal-blue M.

Awaiting Stiles' reply in his office, Blodgett sighed nervously. He wondered if this Dec. 23 breakthrough might save the post-Christmas trip to Antigua he'd promised Gwen and the kids; they so needed it, all of them, including (thought Blodgett, though he had no way to be sure) Timmy. Especially Tim.

A half-mile away on the vast Mega-ware campus, Stiles hunched over his jet-black keyboard, stabbing the keys:

dan: just reviewed your e-mail. have no doubt your finagle of the high-memory problem is elegant. what i'm having doubts about is your grasp of business reality. T-99 isn't just a theoretical code-writing exercise; it's a repositioning of our signature brand. the point here is revenue. why IN THE WORLD would we want T-99 "to mesh seamlessly with T-95," or "purr on original Pentium"? why do you think all our chattel in the industry put up with our strong-arm tactics? because every time we roll out a new Thresholds, we make them a pot of money; the cybersheep scramble to buy

THEIR stuff to make our new stuff hum. why fix old bugs if it'll cost you new revenue? i'm disappointed; i thought you were really smart. now I wonder. you and your team better get on track and get me a beta version by Jan. 1. Q

Each letter of Stiles' e-mail pounded Blodgett's retina like a typewriter key striking vellum. *Really smart* was Stiles' favorite phrase, his highest accolade. Blodgett almost felt his temples bruise as the laurel was yanked from his head.

And Antigua — what about that? Gwen would be so. . . . He typed a panicky reply to Stiles.

■

Stiles read the words in a cold rage. He ran a hand through his lank brown hair, leaving some of it helter-skelter over his high forehead. His angular features narrowed, hawklike, as his lumpy torso leaned forward to type:

blodgett, have you gone idiotic on me? christmas? you've screwed up a product that I'm counting on for a billion dollars in sales next year, and you don't want your vacation disturbed? take Christmas morning off, if you must, but I want you back on task before the eggnog's warm. your team will see me in conference room c at 10 sharp Dec. 26.

French horns stirred the first movement of the Eroica as Stiles noticed the blue M rotating on a computer screen to his left, signaling an e-mail from the outside world. He called it up. Lord, that dimwit from Vanity Fair again. A rephrased query about why Stiles didn't give more to charity. The Richest Man in the History of the World stabbed out a reply: *As I've explained, it takes as much thought to give money away smartly as to make it. I can't do both to my satisfaction at once. When I'm done making money, I'll give it away with the same energy and intelligence I brought to making it.*

Clicking Send, Stiles thought: *As if the joy of making money would ever pale.* He called for the limo; it was time to head home.

The limo snaked through the work-weary, mall-bound traffic (just one more shopping day!), past office parks speckled with twinkling lights, suburban mansions decked in green garland.

Home was 25 minutes away and $40 million in the making. It was an S-shaped palace of solitary pleasures, decreed by Stiles down to the tiniest detail, a compendium of every known idea for enlisting computers in the service of idiosyncratic comfort. At the top of the S, a curved wall of one-way glass threw Cherry Creek Lake's image back out over the water. Otherwise, no windows interrupted the sinuous concrete.

Unfolding his ungainly frame from the limo, Stiles strode to the front door, attaching a small pin to his lapel. This was the signature chip, a maze of microscopic circuits that encoded his every preference and announced them to each room of his house as he entered. As Stiles made his solitary progress through the serpentine house, each room's heat, lighting, wall-projected art and piped-in music adjusted to his presence. After he passed through, the rooms fell dim and silent. Stiles had no flesh-and-blood household staff; he preferred servants made of silica and managed by code. They met his whims smartly, without question or complaint.

Reaching his bedroom, Stiles wriggled out of his gray, droopy cable-knit sweater and tossed it onto the bed — not any ordinary bed, you may rest assured. Its instrument panel rivaled a fighter jet's; with it, Stiles could adjust the bed into 36 positions; monitor the security system; control the 20-speaker sound system, two high-definition TVs, two voice-activated speaker phones (one for international calls, one for domestic) and an experimental 128-bit video game player; and, with the push of a button, release a state-of-the-art PC from a walnut cabinet next to the bed.

Which, flopping onto the circular mattress, Stiles now did. 'Twas time for the spider to survey his web. Though only a few elite Mega-ware managers knew it, Stiles' office and home PCs had absolute access to every cranny of the corporation's PC network, no matter what security walls employees built. Nightly, Stiles would poke into odd corners, perusing memos in the making, chuckling over the ill-advised romantic e-mail, scanning for any signs of worker sloth or rebellion (though payment in options for Mega-ware's ever-rising stock kept those to a minimum). This cyber-spying fueled the "Stiles omniscience" that Mega-ware drones held in awe.

"Let's see . . ." Stiles bit his lip. "I wonder who's begging Erica from Game Development to go for coffee today." He pecked at the charcoal-gray keys.

But the screen did not jump to the lissome Erica's home page on the Mega-ware intranet. As Stiles squinted, it went dark except for one bright point of light, which seemed to spiral forward slowly, growing into the image of a human face. A familiar face.

"What the deuce!" The software mogul's fingers rifled commands at the potent microprocessor, a blizzard of tactics to thwart those computer gremlins called viruses. Futile. The face, familiar and terrifying, gazed out with sad amusement, an eyebrow arching. Stiles, his pasty face debating whether to go red with rage or white with terror, punched and repunched Control+Alt+Delete, trying to reboot.

"Quentin, Quentin," the face spoke. "I thought surely you'd be happier to see me."

"Simon?!" Stiles murmured, fingers now still.

"Yes, Q, it is I." Simon Charles that would be, Stiles' longtime second-in-command, co-weaver of every cunning tactic of market dominance that had bloated Mega-ware Inc.'s coffers. Simon Charles, dead these last seven months, killed skiing in the Andes after a helicopter had deposited him and six others at the top of a remote, thrilling Chilean peak.

The Richest Man in the History of the World summoned his self-possession. "OK, this is fantastically clever, whoever you are," Stiles said into the screen. "And right after your tongue-lashing for playing such a macabre trick on the boss, you get a bonus and six months to make this gimmick marketable."

"Ah, Quentin, the magic here is far beyond the ken of any Megadrone, no matter how smart," the face said. "I've been sent here to give you fair warning of what's to come, in this room, this night."

"Sent? Warning? This is preposterous. Simon Charles died seven months ago in a skiing accident."

"Not accident, Quentin. Suicide. Yes, Quentin, I knew full well I wasn't skier enough for that peak. I fell behind on purpose, then skied off a cliff into what I thought would be oblivion. About that, I was wrong. So wrong.

"You know, I'm feeling cramped. Could you push Alt-F4, Q?"

"Alt-F4? Why?"

"Q, just do it." Stiles did. Charles' face seemed to rise off the screen, float briefly over the bed, then transform into a life-size 3-D hologram, sitting at the foot of the bed.

"There, that's better," Charles said, twitching his shoulders and stretching. The hologram beckoned Stiles, who stumbled across the bed quilt, clutched at the shimmering image, squeezed only air, then fell backward on the bed, glasses askew.

"Wh..., wh...?" Stiles gathered himself. "Why did you do it, Simon? You were smart, respected, rich, powerful. Your life was full."

"Full?" Charles smiled wanly. "No, Q, empty, empty and cold, so cold at the center. Like your life, Q. I had to learn my folly the hardest way. Learn this, Q: To accumulate is to squander, to share is to grow. God wants your icy soul to learn that, without paying the price I have. That's why I've come, to herald to you the ones to follow."

"Who? What ones?"

"Just wait, Quentin. In short time, they'll arrive. As for me, my duty done, I return to the gray territory where I do penance for my folly."

The hologram shrank to a pinprick of intense light, which fled to the monitor, pulsated, then disappeared. On the screen appeared the smiling photo of Erica from Game Development. Stiles, still staring at the foot of the bed, didn't notice.

Disk 2: The First Virus

For a long while after Simon's — what? ghost? hologram? — had gone, Quentin Stiles sat numbly on his bed in his Denver mansion. Finally, shortly after midnight, as if reaching for a teddy bear, he summoned the Thresholds desktop to the monitor of his bedside computer. He gazed at the familiar display, his brainchild, as if it were the Rosetta stone to the universe's hieroglyphs.

Suddenly, a sprig of holly, forest green and merriest red, appeared on the screen. Slowly it spiraled, growing with each revolution. A scent of evergreen tickled Stiles' nose just as a reedy voice, tinged with melancholy and magnolia, filled the room. "Quentin, Alt-F4, please."

As he'd done with the same request from Simon, he complied.

The hologram that assembled at the end of the bed this time was of a man Stiles didn't know: tall, wire-rims, salt-and-pepper beard, eyes flecked with gray and wisdom. He wore a white choir robe; from the rope tied about his trim waist hung an odd assortment — slide rule, protractor, pocket calculator and floppy disk. In the crook of an arm he held a beaded contraption — an abacus, Stiles recognized with a start.

"And you are?"

"The Virus of Christmas Past, Mr. Stiles. The good Simon alerted you to my advent, I trust?"

"In a manner, yes. The Virus, eh? Cute, real cute." Inside Stiles, intellect wrestled fear. The combat left him mordant. "And I suppose now's the point where you show me scenes from my past to teach the error of my grasping ways? And in a nanosecond I'm transformed into the next coming of Mother Teresa?"

"Just so. So you're ready to begin, Mr. Stiles?" The Virus snapped his ghostly fingers; Stiles had no sooner registered the absurdity of the soundless gesture than he noticed that his nocturnal cocoon has been transformed. Some virtual reality trick was being played. His high-tech bedroom was gone, supplanted by a three-dimensional vision of a cinder-block room — a garage in fact — strewn with green-and-white printouts, monitors, fat binders, circuit boards, empty pizza boxes, half-drunk Dos Equis bottles, screwdrivers, and pencils with the erasers chewed.

Stiles knew at once the place and time: Jeff Israel's garage, just outside San Jose, 1976. Stiles walked to a table, looked down. There it was, his first desktop computer, a pokey Conestoga of a processor built from a kit, honored now in the lore of computing a bit like Orville and Wilbur's first flying machine was in aviation. Stiles noticed two young men lounging on a battered sofa, oblivious to him. It was Jeff — and himself, both at age 22.

"Hot damn!" Jeff said, pulling on a beer. "Damn thing works. It works!"

"Yep," the young Q said, smugly, hands behind head.

"You know what this means?" Jeff asked.

"Yep. We're rich."

From Jeff, a blank stare. "Well, yeah, maybe. But what's way cool is what this can do for the average guy, the average community. Computing power that fits on a desktop, at the service of the individual and the grassroots, not just the government, the military, the corporation. No muss, no fuss, no stacks of computer cards. Just type in a few commands and go. We did it, brother. We can make these little processors stand up and say Mama. Think of it, networks of these things, one in every house, people writing instant letters to each other on it, letters to their congressman, to City Hall. Democracy like Jefferson visualized it, man. Awesome."

"You on drugs, Israel?" young Quentin asked. "Well, of course you are, but that's no excuse to babble so. Look, friend, this electronic brain we just taught to talk is a business machine. It's built to tote up the profit and the loss, inventory and orders, in about a thousandth of the time the drones in white shirts do it now. A business machine, of most interest to the 800-pound gorilla thereof, IBM. We get Big Blue to put this operating system in its boxes, and we've got it made in the shade, brother."

"Q, Q, you're thinking small, man. This could transform society; it could alter history. Using our language, computers could turn every clerk into a philosopher, a king."

"Israel, the only people I want to transform is us, from broke nerds into rich inventors. If you'll excuse me" — he flopped his size 12s on the floor — "I'm going to look up IBM's phone number."

Looking on, Stiles could almost feel how, at that moment, his polyester shirt had itched his expanding midriff. Then, the scene was gone. Back in his bedroom, Stiles sensed an expectant look from the Virus of Christmas past.

"What?" Stiles said, combative, palms extended upward. "I was right, wasn't I? Ol' Israel, clueless then, clueless to the end."

Peeved, the Virus waved his abacus in the air.

A new virtual reality. A corporate boardroom, the scene played out soundlessly, as if someone had hit the mute button. Israel making feverish gestures, pounding a blackboard with his chalk, a tableful of pinstripes and wingtips looking on; young Stiles sitting, rubbing his temples, wincing. Israel storming out, the suits turning to Stiles. From Stiles, a nod, a handshake. The tableau froze on the handshake.

The room went black. Stiles spoke to the dark: "C'mon, what was I supposed to do? They didn't want Jeff in any deal. He was unstable, on the edge of blowing it. He wasn't acting smart."

Stiles heard the whispered drawl from behind him: "And what did Jeff do a month later, Quentin? Killed himself, didn't he? Seems to be the price of being your partner, eh? And that silly vision of his? Seems millions of others had the same one, invented something called the Internet to give it birth. A little slow to figure that out, weren't you, Quentin? But you recovered with a vengeance, didn't you? As you always do, when there's money to be made."

Stiles offered a wry smile: "Hey, thanks."

The Virus sighed. "I see I can't complete this night's work. I must make way for another. Farewell, Quentin Stiles. Learn — if you can."

Again the hologram dissolved to a point of light, which danced to the screen and disappeared. Again, Stiles' favorite intranet photo of Erica from Game Development grinned becomingly from the screen.

Uneasy, Stiles bid her farewell, punched up his official biography, as presented at www.mega-ware.com. He reread its consoling version of his visionary partnership with IBM. So lost in pleasant nostalgia was Stiles that it took a moment for him to notice that the holly had returned to the screen. Wordlessly, Stiles punched Alt-F4.

He turned to see a hologram of a smiling woman sitting on the bed's edge, a lovely redhead, long legs crossed, dressed in elegant green silk.

"Mr. Stiles" — a slim hand extended in greeting — "the Virus of Christmas Present, at your service."

Disk 3: The Second Virus

"Erica?" Quentin Stiles said in wonderment to the shimmering hologram of his young employee, which had just materialized in his bedroom, announcing itself as the Virus of Christmas Present.

"Not in the flesh, so to speak," the hologram replied to the Richest Man in the History of the World, who tugged busily at his shirt and smoothed his unkempt hair. "She'd be amazed, though, to know you recognize her. In fact, the first place we shall go is a little impromptu holiday party she and some friends in Game Development are having at McGillicuddy's." The hologram-Erica gestured gracefully, splinters of light leaping from her bracelets.

As it had twice before this night, Stiles' bedroom morphed, this time into a chain bistro replete with the usual ferns, Tiffany lamps, high-backed booths and kitschy wall clutter. A group of young mega-ware Inc. software designers bunched merrily around a table littered with half-full pitchers and nachos crumbs. Erica, Stiles noticed as he inched closer to the group, sat next to a tanned, square-jawed young fellow.

"Ya' know," Square Jaw said boisterously to no one in particular, "call me a stone geek, but I love Christmas. Out with my fellow serfs to get faced in honor of the day, then tomorrow morning I hop a plane, head home to 'rent land and surprise my mom with all the loot I can buy her, thanks to my lucrative serfdom. It's a wonderful life." He stood, raised his mug theatrically: "Merry Christmas and God bless us, everyone, especially ol' Darth Stiles, he of the dark jowls and the helium stock."

Mugs clinked and jostled; amid titters Stiles was toasted with samples from his huge portfolio of in-house nicknames: "To Darth! . . . To Q-Tip! . . . The Wizard of Odd! . . . Control-All-Da-Geek!"

"Erica," Square Jaw turned to her. "You do not salute our dark lord and master."

"Y-y-y-shhhhh," Erica said with a shudder. "I can't. He gives me the whim-whams, lurking up in his lair all hunched up, writing us e-mails 24 hours a day, never talking to anyone face to face, watching us from on high with that I'm-smarter-than-you ego. He's like a Vulcan who did a mind-meld with a hard drive." Hoots and high fives around the table.

"But Erica, my love, he's making us all rich."

"Yes, and as soon as I can, I'm gonna take the money and run to a place where I can work for a human being, not a master android with greasy hair."

"Ouch!" Square Jaw yelled. "Hear that, Q? Erica says: Try the Herbal Essence."

Quentin did hear it, standing by the virtual bistro's door with pursed lips.

"Fun party," the Virus-Erica observed. Stiles, downcast, chewed his lower lip. "Ready for another visit?" the green-clad apparition asked. "Either way, here goes."

Suddenly Stiles stood before a suburban home, warm brick and mullioned windows, prim topiary framing the front entrance. The Virus opened the virtual door and beckoned. They went up the central staircase to the master bedroom. There, open suitcases were scattered about, half-packed — or was it half-emptied? Gwen Blodgett sat on the side of the bed, elbows on knees, minutely examining her nails. Dan stood, one shoe in hand, by an open closet door.

"Gwen, I . . . I . . . I . . ."

"That's right, Dan," Gwen said. "You can't think of anything to say but I, I, I."

"That's not fair, Gwen. I have no choice."

Her pageboy swirled as her head jerked toward him, fierce eyes boring in: "No choice? No choice! You have many choices; you just pretend you don't. You choose to let that tyrant rule you. You choose to put your work in front of your family. You choose to pretend that what I and Adam and . . . and Timmy want from you is what your workaholism can buy us. It's not, Dan. It's you we want, whether or not your name ends up on the Thresholds 99 manual. What we want is you in Antigua with us, not here dancing on Quentin Stiles' strings."

"Look, sweetie, you guys go. If this meeting the day after Christmas goes OK, maybe I can fly down for a couple days."

"Sure, Dan. Maybe you will. Likely you won't. Either way, the kids spend Christmas without their dad. And when Tim . . ." — Gwen swallowed hard — ". . . when Tim sees the ocean, when I see whether this crazy idea is going to work, his father, the only person who can reach him now, won't be there. He'll be pecking away at a keyboard, trying to make Quentin Stiles another billion to go with the other 80. You talk about no choice. Let me show you no choice!"

Gwen sprang from the bed like a cougar, dug nails into her husband's wrist and began to drag him out of the room. "Gwen," he cried out. "Don't."

"Come look at your son, then."

"Gwen . . ." Resigned, Dan trudged into Timmy's room. The curly haired 10-year-old sat cross-legged on a chair in a fluffy Power Rangers robe. He stared into the monitor of a sleek PC. But his hands weren't on the keyboard. They clutched his side as he rocked back and forth, back and forth, back and forth. Finally, his right hand reached out stiffly for the mouse; he rolled and clicked for a few seconds. The complex geometrical pattern on the screen shifted into a Jackson Pollock-like swirl of colors. Timmy's arms retracted, clutched his torso; the rocking resumed. His parents stood still in the doorway, watching, not touching.

Stiles turned to the hologram. "I remember this kid. He was into the office once, showed me a Web page he'd been designing. Damned impressive; kid was only 7 or 8. I told Blodgett we'd have to sign Tim up before somebody else got him. Nice boy. What's going on? What's wrong with him?"

"Are you just curious, Quentin, or do you really care?"

"I . . . I care."

"Tim has a gift for computers besides which his father's pales — as does yours, Quentin. Dan Blodgett, of course, was delighted when Tim first showed signs, even before kindergarten. He worked with him, bought him the best gear. Meanwhile, Tim was also a regular little boy:

Power Rangers, Legos, soccer in the fall, Little League in the spring. Last year, though, it began to change. He spent more and more time in his room, on the computer, designing programs, GUIs, browsers, you name it. No more cartoons, no more sports. He became withdrawn, rarely slept. Gwen and Dan tried it all: specialists, shrinks, medication. Nothing helped. It was like watching one of those slow-motion falls in the movies. Only this wasn't a stunt man falling into a huge pillow. This was their son falling into a kind of high-tech autism, their son being swallowed inch by inch by the computer."

"What's the situation now?"

"You see it. Tim spends all day in front of his PC. About six months ago, Dan figured out that Tim had written his own, private programming language; he could talk all day to the computer, and no one else could 'listen.' So Dan watched for hours on end, studied printouts, began to break the code. He tries to talk to Tim using his special code; the boy will respond, sometimes, but the next time Dan tries, he finds Tim's rewritten the code, made it more complex, inserted dead-ends. It's eternal cat-and-mouse."

Stiles' hand raked his hair, his eyes locked on Tim's rocking figure.

"What was his wife saying about the ocean?"

"Tim always loved the ocean. The last time he seemed his old self was their trip to Antigua last year, playing tag with the waves, Frisbee with his brother, laughing. They thought he was coming out of it. Then, after their return, the rocking began. So, Antigua — Gwen hoped maybe it held some magic."

"And I . . ."

"Ruined it, Quentin."

"Well, why didn't Blodgett tell me? Why didn't he

explain?"

"He tried, but you slapped him down."

"Wait a minute. He never mentioned Timmy."

"Would you, if you were he? Ask sympathy for personal pain from the man of pure brain? Come now, Quentin."

"Maybe I can help. Maybe help Blodgett break through the code."

"Interesting challenge for the world's smartest man, eh?"

Stiles winced. "Well, yes, but it's not just that. This is just terrible. I . . . I never thought of a PC as . . . as wounding a child this way. We have to turn this around, we just have to. That poor woman . . ."

Stiles looked from the rocking boy to the doorway. There, his parents stood. Dan's hand reached for his wife's, his fingers fumbling to lock with hers. After a second's hesitation, her hand clenched his.

Disk 4: The Third Virus

Quentin Stiles' eyes were clenched shut, trying to erase the sight of two parents gazing in anguish as their son rocked to and fro before a computer screen, locked in autistic embrace of a binary world that didn't include them.

When the software mogul opened his eyes, the scene was indeed gone. As was the hologram of the lovely Erica, the Virus of Christmas Present who had brought him that vision of the sorrowful home of his employee Dan Blodgett.

Stiles knew his holiday lore well enough to suspect that a third hologram ought to follow the others. Staring at the computer screen that had this night proven fertile with wonders, he waited, emptied of all emotions but two most foreign to him: regret and sadness. That poor kid, Timmy.

After a while, the spiraling sprig of holly that had heralded the other two viruses appeared on the screen. Dutifully, Stiles punched Alt-F4, to release the virus from the box. An angular figure, draped in a black robe, face in shadow, materialized at the foot of Stiles' bed. With a touch of annoyance, Stiles noted how much it looked like the evil emperor from Star Wars. It seemed undignified, the Richest Man in the History of the World awaiting enlightenment from a George Lucas cliche.

"The Virus of Christmas Future, I presume?" Stiles asked.

A slight incline of the robed head.

"Less talkative than the others, I see. Well, go ahead, back to the future with me." Stiles' forced jauntiness evaporated. "First, what about the boy, Tim? Show me what becomes of him."

Another nod of the head, a slow wave of a cloaked arm.

To Stiles' rapt attention, the bedroom of Dan and Gwen Blodgett returned. Stiles' eyes gobbled details of the scene; a desk calendar showed the year 2010. The decade had treated the couple shockingly. Dan was gray and gaunt; Gwen's eyes were dark hollows.

"Sure you won't come, Dan?"

"I can't, sweetie; I just can't. I can't bear to see him in that place."

"We're his parents, Dan; we can't just abandon him."

"I haven't," Dan said fiercely. "Gwen, we each reach out to him as best we can. For you, it's the touch of your hand. For me, it's that damn keyboard over there. Sometimes, when I'm fighting the labyrinths he weaves inside the computer with his special code, I can almost feel him waiting on the other side of a virtual wall, waiting for me to break through, wanting me to. And not wanting. I get so close, but then he scurries away. He's a genius, Gwen. I can barely track his scent inside this cyberworld he's built."

"I know, Dan, I know. Finish zipping me up, and I'll go."

Stiles' hands plowed through his greasy hair. "Virus, why couldn't I change this? I've got billions to spend, the best programming brains in the universe. We should have gotten through to this child. Certainly we should have."

The robed figure glided to Stiles' bedside terminal, typed briefly. Stiles took in the screen's one sentence: *If you change input, you can change output.*

"OK, OK, good, this future is not inevitable. That's good; that's good." His hands rubbed together. Then a cloud passed over Stiles' visage.

"And me, Virus? What happens to me, to Mega-ware Inc., to Thresholds and Net-a-gator and the rest?"

The scene seemed to spill out of the robed hologram's

pointed finger.

A warm, well-appointed living room, Early American style, Shaker tables, Amish quilts, a Christmas tree strung with popcorn and candy canes by a fireplace. A dozen people, six couples by the look of it, sitting in a circle, talking animatedly about a novel. Stiles struggled to parse the dialogue; Barkis, Steerforth, Micawber — the names tumbled by, jogging dimmed memories. Wait, that's it, Dickens, David Copperfield.

"What's this got to do with me, Virus?" No reply. Stiles scanned the room. A digital clock-calendar sat on an end table: Dec. 23, 2010.

"That's odd," Stiles mused out loud. "Where's the Big Box in this house? By this time, convergence should be well-established. Interactive movies on demand; worldwide video links. Why are they just sitting around talking?"

Stiles strolled to the kitchen, where a humble portable TV sat on a counter. In the family room, a large bookcase, but no screen. In the office, ah, there was a tower PC system, with a 17-inch screen. Ample, but hardly the wall-size panels that convergence had seemed to imply.

"What's up with these folks, Virus? Are they some kind of idiotic hippie Luddites?"

The virtual scene dissolved. The Virus bent over his keyboard, typed again, beckoned Stiles. The Virus had done a Nexus search; a New York Times headline was at the top of the screen. Mega-ware Inc. founder Quentin Stiles dead at 56; car crash climaxes fall from Olympian heights. The date was Dec. 23, 2010.

His throat thick, Stiles grasped the mouse to scroll down:

"Quentin Stiles, whose software genius and ruthless business sense catapulted him to fabulous riches by the time he was 30, died yesterday in a car accident in Des Moines, Iowa. At his death, while still one of the world's 10 richest people, he was in many ways a broken, bitter man, emblem, for many, of the arrogance and false hype of the Early Computer Age."

"This can't be; what claptrap," Stiles yelped, but read on. The awful account scrolled by: the consumer revolt against the bug-laden Thresholds 99; the rise of brash challengers to Mega-ware's dominance; the rash of successful antitrust suits against the Stiles colossus; the repeated failures to anticipate which direction the Internet would jump; the mass defections of talent; the plummet in stock price. And something else . . .

Most surprising, dramatic and perhaps damaging of all was how Mr. Stiles became the dark avatar, the rallying symbol of a protest movement against the corporate vision of convergence. The movement scathingly rejected the bid for work-and-leisure dominance made by the Big Box, that hybrid of computer and television on which Mega-ware, and many others, had placed their bets.

"This movement, dubbed High-Touch, took as its credo an acronym: L.O.B. (standing for Live Outside the Box). By

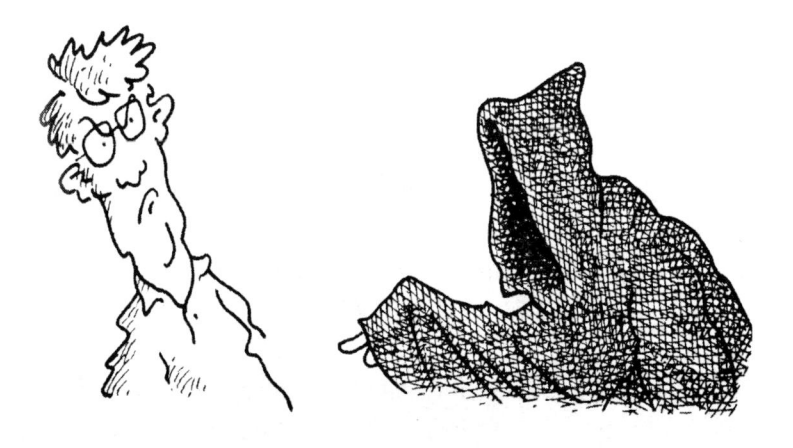

2005, the letters L.O.B. could be seen everywhere in the United States, on bumper stickers, coffee mugs, colorful flags flying outside suburban homes. LOBsters, as they became known, advocate what they call right relations with technology. They run 12-step programs to free people of addiction to television; seek to redefine the computer as a tool of community and family, not capitalism; advocate conversation and reading of books off-line as the best recreation.

"To say High-Touch has swept America would be hyperbole, but it has become influential, particularly in turning public opinion against its betes noires, Mr. Stiles and Mega-ware Inc. Many pinpoint Mr. Stiles' 2002 televised interview with Katie Couric, in which he angrily denounced LOBsters as 'idiotic Luddite hippies,' as the pivotal moment in Mega-ware's stunning fall from grace."

Stiles' pale face looked up. "This is a joke, right?" From the Virus, a jagged silence. Stiles looked back at the screen; on it, the message had returned: *If you change input, you can change output.*

Then the screen, the room, Stiles' consciousness — all went dark.

Disk 5: The End of It

Stiles awoke around 7 a.m. Dec. 24, though no whisper of branches, call of bird, or ray of sun could have signaled the morning hour to him in the high-tech cocoon where he slept. A digital readout by the bed in his Denver mansion told the Richest Man in the History of the World the time of day.

"Whew, what a weird dream," he murmured, running a hand through the dull brown hair that stood at attention like a clump of sloppy soldiers. Thank God, he thought, all that nonsense about Viruses of Christmas Past and Future, about autistic kids and Luddites wasn't real.

He spied his gray cable-knit sweater in a heap on the floor. Boy, he'd been more tired than he'd thought, to just fall asleep after shucking the sweater.

Time to check the Asian markets. Stiles swung the screen of his bedside computer toward him, expecting to see the image of Erica from Game Development, on whose intranet page he'd been noodling when he drifted off.

Instead, the screen pierced him with the words "If you change input, you can change output." He looked to the foot of his massive circular bed; on the rumpled bedclothes lay three sprigs of holly, tokens left by the viruses.

"No!" Stiles shuddered. Inside him, a dozen small deaths gave way to a slow, hard birth of resolve.

"Timmy," he said out loud, firmly, then pulled his keyboard toward him. There had to be a way to tap into the home computer where Dan Blodgett's autistic son wove his cunning, lonely, binary world.

His thinking suddenly clear, muscular, urgent, Stiles typed and clicked, typed and clicked, for hours, pausing from time to time to chew his lip and stare at the screen.

Around noon, he shouted in triumph, "Got it!" He jumped to his feet, pumped his arm like a pitcher who had just finished a no-hitter, and did a little jig about the bed. He stored his work on a floppy and pulled on his sweater. Got to get to the Blodgetts.

He headed for the doorway, then turned and ran back to the PC, giggling in excitement. He punched out an e-mail, to the Vanity Fair writer whose queries about charitable giving he'd put off irritably the night before:

Stiles here. Ignore e-mail of last night. I'd like to share my new plans to form the Stiles Foundation. Will be endowed with half, no, make that three-quarters of my Mega-ware stock. First grants: $1 billion for research into autism. $1 billion to America's libraries, to ensure equal community access to Internet — and to replenish inventory of classic works in bound volume. $1 billion to WebRoots, a program of challenge grants to grassroots groups to figure out how to use computers to further community and democracy. Details TK; gotta go. Q.

One more quick e-mail, for circulation on the Mega-ware intranet: *Happy holidays. An announcement: In the new year, I'll be starting a program of informal lunches with employees called "Q and You." Just a chance to talk in a casual setting (McGillicuddy's?) about your hopes and dreams and how Mega-ware Inc. can help you reach them. Looking forward to it . . . Q.*

In his kitchen, sipping coffee that had automatically brewed when sensors in his bed signaled he'd risen, Stiles called out to the hidden speakerphone, "Local call. Dial ..." Then he hesitated. Why disturb his chauffeur on Christmas Eve? He'd drive himself to the Blodgetts'.

Stiles didn't really know the way, but the sunny, crisp day was so delightful, he didn't bother with the navigation computer. He puzzled his way around suburban streets, delighting in the bright wreaths, the UPS packages sitting on doorsteps bearing late-arriving treasures for beneath the tree.

After stopping twice to chatter excitedly with gas-station attendants about where 234 Dorritt Lane might be, he found the home of Dan and Gwen Blodgett. Ignoring the doorbell, he pounded heartily on the door, right beneath the evergreen wreath with the real candy canes. He pulled off one striped cane and was licking it when the door opened.

Gwen Blodgett's bloodshot eyes widened: "M-Mr. Stiles?" Her voice was edged with shock on one side, contempt on the other. "What can I do for you?"

"Let me in first, Gwen," Stiles said with mock sternness. "I have something to tell that husband of yours."

"Mr. Stiles." The tone was steel. "This is our home; we are having a hard day with our holiday plans spoiled. As you know. Is this really necessary?"

Before Stiles could reply, Dan came scuffling downstairs. "Who is it, Gwen? . . . Q! Mr. Stiles, I'm . . . uh . . .

sorry, uh, come in, yes, come in."

Stiles took the opening: "Blodgett, I've something to say, so hear me out. I've been an ass, a perfect jerk. Have you canceled that trip to Antigua yet? Darn! Well, no problem. It's back on; I'll make new reservations. The whole trip is on me. And about Thresholds, you're right; it's time we put out a perfected product that doesn't cost in real terms 10 times the price on the box. If we don't, sooner or later consumers will turn on us. So give the whole team the rest of the year off; we'll reconvene Jan. 2. You go to Antigua and make sure Timmy gets plenty of ocean time ..."

If Dan Blodgett had just seen the ghost of his dead father, he couldn't have been more slack-jawed. But his wife peered acutely at Stiles.

"Timmy? How do you know about Tim, Mr. Stiles?"

"That's not important now. What's important is, I have an idea how we might break through to his world, Dan. Been at it for hours. Dying to give it a try. Is he here, Gwen? Can I give it a try?"

As if sleepwalking, Dan Blodgett gestured to the staircase and followed Stiles and Gwen up.

Tim sat cross-legged, rocking silently in front of his computer.

"Mind if I cut in, Tim?" Stiles chuckled heartily, then pulled the black floppy disk out of his coat pocket, slipped it into the drive.

Tim's father regained speech: "Q, what's that? What are you doing? He ... he doesn't respond, you know."

"Well," Stiles said with an eager grin, clicking the mouse. "Let's just see about that."

A new swirl of color on the screen seemed to catch Tim's eye. His arms reached out stiffly to the keyboard, remained poised a half-inch above the keys. The colors resolved themselves into words and numbers, a kind of code. Tim's right index finger punched *Enter*. A new pattern of hues, assembling into a new coded message. Again Tim's finger stroked the key: *Enter*. On it went like this, for agonizing, exhilarating minutes. Stiles stood by Tim, murmuring, "That's it, yes; that's a boy; good, Tim, excellent." Dan and Gwen hugged each other around the shoulders, mystified, dazzled.

One more Enter, and the screen filled with video images of an ocean, blue-green waves foaming onto a pink beach. Tim's legs uncrossed, felt shakily for the floor. He leaned forward; his fingers caressed the screen, following the ebb and eddy of the waves. Stiles reached down, clicked twice.

Tim leaned back, looked intently at the keyboard, punched a key. The screen went bright blue. Slowly, Tim typed: *Y . . . E . . . S*. The screen went dark; in the silence, they could hear the disk drive whirring to a stop.

Tim half-turned in the chair. After a blank instant, his eyes seemed to focus; a tiny smile fumbled for purchase on his lips.

He looked up at his mother and father.

"Hi, Mom," he said. "Hey, Dad, want to go outside and have a catch?"

About the Authors

Chris Satullo is Editorial Page Editor of The Philadelphia Inquirer. He was named to the post in March 2000 after serving six years as the page's deputy editor. Before joining The Inquirer in 1989, he spent 13 years at The Express newspaper in Easton, Pa., where he was assistant managing editor and a syndicated columnist. He has won more than 30 awards for reporting, editorials, columns, civic journalism and newspaper design. He is married with two children and lives in Lafayette Hill, Pa.

Tony Auth has been editorial cartoonist for The Inquirer since 1971. He has won the Pulitzer Prize for cartooning, as well as five Overseas Press Club Awards and the Sigma Delta Chi for Distinguished Service in Journalism. His political cartoons are distributed in this country and abroad by the Universal Press Syndicate. He is the author and/or illustrator of several books for children, including "The Sky of Now" and "The Tree of Here" by Chaim Potok. He is married with two children and lives in Lower Merion, Pa.

The Newspaper That Fits In Your Pocket

Crisis on the Coast
The risky development of America's shores

Beyond the Flames
One toxic dump, two decades of sorrow

Philly's Final Four
Complete coverage of the 2000 NCAA Women's Basketball Final Four.

Lost at Sea
The true story of ten fisherman battling icy water off the Jersey shore

A Christmas Quartet
Four modern tales of the holiday

FAQ
Sound answers for real computing questions

Order them at http://inkspot.philly.com
or by calling 1-215-854-4444